Charlotte Ritchie is a new author living outside of Calgary, Alberta. Her own struggles with finding self-achievement and career success were supplemented using fictional writing as a form of stress relief. It has been the move to retirement from a career in the oil industry that has allowed her the time and resources to share her story with the world.

To my wonderful friends for reading and editing my work.

To Lyall and Karen for telling me to take a chance.

And to Eric for telling me I was worth the chance.

Life is nothing without each and every one of you!

Charlotte Ritchie

WEEKEND PIPELINE TO LOVE AND ROMANCE

AUSTIN MACAULEY PUBLISHERS™

LONDON · CAMBRIDGE · NEW YORK · SHARJAH

A CIP catalogue record for this title is available from the British Library.

ISBN 9781398485198 (Paperback)
ISBN 9781398485204 (ePub e-book)

www.austinmacauley.co.uk

First Published 2024
Austin Macauley Publishers Ltd®
1 Canada Square
Canary Wharf
London
E14 5AA

I wish to acknowledge my family and friends for the love, strength, and encouragement to write this story. I am blessed to have their support to follow my dream of writing. I am thankful to all the resources through Austin Macauley Publishers in professionally bringing my story to the public.

Chapter 1
Miami, FL

The last bite of Betty's grilled grouper was likely one bite too much. But the treat of a lunch, out for business was not to be ignored. When the general manager sent the meeting request to her calendar, she accepted. Business talk had been largely concluded prior to the server placing their steaming catch of the day, as ordered at each place setting. The lead developer and engineer had arrived first and grabbed a table on the outside deck to enjoy being out of the office. While they were both enjoying sitting in the sunshine for an hour, the server had been most considerate to ensure, the shade of the table umbrella was continually adjusted for her to remain shaded.

From their first team encounter, they had seen a small young woman, who was; abundantly clear on business, had the ability to succeed and help others succeed, was firmly reluctant to be in direct sunlight except when walking, and held a firm rejection for any personal relationships with staff, other than positive working friendships. Both men had asked this small dynamo of a lady for drinks and dinner, and were both clearly rejected in spite of, both of their general success with the opposite sex. Also, they had both found out very clearly that should a spot in the sun be the only option for a team meal, she would speak with the staff herself and even a manager if necessary to be moved under shade or have suitable coverage provided.

Elizabeth (Betty) McDowall could not believe that she was currently living and working in Miami, Florida. As a project manager for software product development and implementation she never dreamed of having an assignment that allowed her to enjoy a lunch served in the sunshine 12 months of the year. Although her skin had picked up a light kiss from the sun, she was not interested in tanning for personal reasons. Only the hint of colour took her northern, pale skin tone and turned it into a healthy glow and certainly not a tan.

The grocery store and a deli near her condo allowed the purchase of ingredients for most meals and Betty was more than happy to take her own lunch as she found she was often so busy, that taking the time to find a food vendor, much less the expense was rarely worth it. However, if a group event was organised, she was always quick to go along, as receiving an invitation made attendance a must. People relaxed over lunch, especially sitting there in the sunshine with wonderful seafood options.

Betty had always known to keep the client relationship strong, and to get to know the people you were working with, especially as a contractor. She had realised that was a skill when entering pre-school and it had served her well through the peer-pressure of high school, study groups in university, to entering the workplace. Understanding wants versus needs was valuable to a project manager, but so was knowing when and how to change your approach to avoid a task or the entire project from going off the rails.

There was a warm breeze coming in off the water. A few clouds in the still cerulean blue sky hinted at a possible afternoon storm. It could mean a walk home after work in the rain, but Betty cared little. She was looking forward to the cloud bringing a hint of pink and orange to the sunset that was enjoyed most evenings from her condo balcony. Right now, she was full from consuming the fresh catch of grouper and was relaxing, listening to the basic conversation of her co-workers planning an evening golf time.

They always asked her to join in, but golf was not something that had ever really held her interest. She had taken lessens, as encouraged by her parents, in the summer at the community golf course. She had even taken golf as a gym class elective in high school, but that was only because her best friend, Julia Marks, had a crush on Jimmy Schultz and he had signed up. Good grief, she thought now, the things we did for friends, and to follow boys.

But now, she was sitting fully satiated with grilled fish, and enjoying the view of the Miami River. Small craft moved along the water, leaving a light ripple in their wake. Rather than seeing that as a disturbance to the glass like shine of the water, instead she saw beautiful shapes of crystal carving images. Betty loved admiring the beautiful creations from the Swarovski crystal makers. She was continually amazed at the unique and detailed items that could be crafted from glass.

Sitting on that sunny patio watching the sparkling water, Betty recalled how she had jumped at the opportunity to come to Florida. Peter Sims, her boyfriend of five years, announced, following dinner on a Thursday night that he had decided, he did not want to ever get married and would move out of their condo by the time she got home from work the next day. Betty was stunned for the first month, going through the motions of daily hygiene and work routine. She lost 10 pounds that month and it had been her best friend Julia, who barged her way into the condo one Saturday morning and made Betty eat. It was also Julia who picked her up at work twice a week and drove her to private counselling appointments.

Julia never asked how each session went, or what was said. She simply sat in the office waiting room, and then would drive Betty back to her office. By the third month, Betty had relieved Julia of her chauffer duties and asked that she resume the role of a friend. Best friends that met for lunch, hair and nail appointments, trips to the mall to stroll, shop and be silly for an afternoon, allowing Betty the opportunity to slowly make her way back into public places.

Betty was already planning on selling the condo, she shared with Peter, when she was asked to come to the reception and sign for an envelope. Peter had retained a lawyer to formally ask for the sale of the condo. Apparently, Peter was getting married to someone else, so wanted a quick sale of their condo to allow him a new home purchase.

Never wanted to get married! Betty knew it was a lie at the announcement of moving out. Not only was Peter a jerk, but he was a coward as well. Everyone had been right; Betty was best to leave Peter in the past without a backward thought. The sun in Florida was the cathartic treatment that was truly helping, as was a demanding project that consumed her every waking moment.

Jeremy Marlin, started out his career with environmental engineering, now 25 years holding a personally rewarding career as general manager of the Miami-Dade Pipelines (MDP), was looking across the table at the lovely young

Project Manager. That small but powerful young lady had been sent by his friend, Bart Hartley, to oversee the implementation of a new software program at MDP. Elizabeth (Betty) McDowall as her resume had read was approved personally by Bart even though her personal details stated she was only 28 years old. Bart had more than assured Jeremy that in spite of her young age, Betty was more than capable of overseeing a successful implementation, and was considered his top Project Manager.

Jeremy had put his trust in Bart to select only top candidates for the implementation team. When Betty followed the MDP receptionist into the boardroom for the initial team meeting, Jeremy had truly thought that she was just another administrative person in training. Betty was just slightly shorter than the receptionist at 5'5". Her slim build gave the impression of someone just out of high school or college at the most. Her hair was brown, but as she moved there was a touch of gold or red depending on the light. It was worn long and straight sitting just past her shoulders with a precisely defined part down the centre of her crown which Jeremy wondered often, if she had measured.

She wore a very plain dress and a light sweater with very plain low-heeled shoes. Her face was soft and round and still, was a pretty girl, she would never be glamorous like many of the young ladies, including his daughters, around Miami. Her make-up was very lightly applied. He was actually encouraged, that they may be getting some staff that would make a career for themselves, rather than filling in time until securing a rich husband.

But that was no administrative trainee and what continued to stun Jeremy to that day was her approach to him, with an outstretched hand anticipating a formal handshake and turning her soft mouth into an engaging and genuine smile and simply stating, "Hello, I'm Betty McDowall, here to ensure we have a successful implementation."

Jeremy remembered being stunned at Betty's appearance. He knew she was young from her CV but was not prepared for someone so small. But Jeremy also recalled how he would go home each evening to have his wife, Susan, who would tease him by asking "How did the kid do today?" He always had to respond, "Brilliant, just brilliant!"

Betty did not date, at least what Jeremy knew of. That was both a blessing in his mind, and a concern. She never dressed like the glamorous Miami clubbing player, her make-up was always perfectly applied with a very light touch, her clothing was simple yet stylish and regardless of how she tried to make herself plain and invisible there was a sparkle in her eyes and even more so, when her smile or laugh was truly from her heart. She was soft in looks and tongue, worked tirelessly to ensure perfection in her work, but was the first to offer assistance and knowledge to any team member struggling.

During the months of the project, both Jeremy and his wife Susan began to see Betty as a daughter figure. So much so, that Jeremy had asked Bart directly if she had left a partner behind. Bart only knew from his secretary that Betty had recently broken up with her boyfriend, but had no actual details. Perhaps that was why Betty accepted that project, to get away and recover. Jeremy's own daughter had moved home for a few months following a breakup, but that was just to get back on her feet and regroup. Now a few years later that same daughter was happily married. He hoped that would be the recovery Betty needed to get back into the dating world. Betty was far too much of a gem to go un-treasured.

Chapter 2
6 Months Earlier in
Albany, NY...

Having placed a call to both her counsellor and friend Julia after a second, still shocked at reading the letter from Peter's lawyer, Betty called her mum to ask if it was possible to have her old room for a few months while the condo was being sold. Her mum not only agreed, but came over that evening to help pack personal items and assist, while leaving the rest for staging the unit during sale. Her dad showed his support by borrowing a truck on Saturday for the transport of personal items. Within 3 days of the lawyer's letter, the condo was on the market and Betty was back in her childhood, single bed, staring at Spice Girls posters colliding with those of Michael Jackson and Prince. Every morning she left the house for work, with a lunch packed by her mum, and a shout out of, "Love you! Call if you will be late for dinner."

"I love you too Mum!" Betty responded, but the tears that formed were huge, thanks to her mum and dad for the unfailing support, she always had for her entire life. However, the regret of a relationship failure was too fresh to ignore. The fact that after 4 years of university and 5 years with Peter, she was again living at home like a wounded animal, licking her wounds and having lost a battle she was not even aware being a part of.

Months following the breakup, she still asked herself what had gone wrong, and still received the same answers from the counsellor, Julia, her parents and even friends of Peter and her as a couple. "You did nothing wrong; Peter is just a jerk."

No one knew this new love of Peter's. She was apparently a lawyer in some New York firm that was assigned to Peter's company 2 years ago. The affair had started the day they met and now the rumour circulating was, that Peter would be moving to Manhattan as Albany was far too limiting for their career aspirations. All Betty felt was foolish. Foolish for not seeing that Peter had such powerful career goals, and doubly foolish for not having a clue of the 2 years affair.

Well, the one place Betty was no fool, was business. On the advice of her counsellor, sunk all her effort into work, and group outings with friends other than just Julia, was a perfect prescription to get her back in good humour at work. The added bonus of this work and social recommitment was, limiting the time spent at home with her parents. Betty was quick to tell Julia, that loving and appreciating her parents for supporting her while the condo sold was separate from going from an adult that lived with another man, to now being back in their home as a child. In short, the condo needed to sell, thus allowing Betty to make her own plans for purchasing something else. Betty knew that it would not be something in the same neighbourhood, or size, but it would be her own, and she would be on her own.

Her added dedication to work did not go unnoticed by her employers. The new release of their pipeline management software, Flow-Soft, came in, not only on time, but on budget, a huge rarity for the software industry. The project team was treated to a celebration spa day and dinner at the owner's private club. Having been pampered, plucked and polished, Betty was relaxing at dinner, having enjoyed her second glass of the best tasting wine ever experienced. No wine connoisseur by any stretch of imagination, she only knew it was red and wonderfully flavourful. Her project teammate Kim Barkley, was quick to point out that the waiter had confirmed that there was not a single bottle of wine at that club under 200 dollars, and that the one being enjoyed was around the 500 dollars range.

Betty immediately felt guilty for having agreed to a second glass, the cost was unbelievable. But it was only moments later when the company owner, Bart Hartley, rose from the table followed by a waiter with ready refills, to walk around the table, refilling each person's glass with a personal word of thanks for their project dedication and skill. Betty was beyond impressed. It was one thing to have pride in your work, to be part of such a team, but it was wonderful to see the company owner showing his thanks in such a personal way.

Following his round of the table, Bart Hartley filled his own glass and provided a very short toast to each member of the Flow-Soft team. Noting how each individual, at every level had provided the integral contributions for a successful software release. "Please enjoy the evening and have the club call your taxi when ready to leave," were his ending words. No one had been allowed to arrive in their own vehicle that day. A chartered limo bus had picked everyone up at their home and everyone would be safely returned home at no personal expense. A very class act in Betty's opinion.

There had been rumours and talk around the office that the new Flow-Soft release was being looked at by many pipeline firms around the country and throughout the world. Some were existing clients, anxious for the upgrade, but the opportunity to sell the product to a new company was always the goal of a new release. So, it was not a big surprise when Betty was called into a meeting to discuss the implementation for a new client. Betty had often assisted with product demonstrations, and suggestions for client usage, but that was different. The client had asked for an onsite implementation team, and Bart was personally asking Betty to be the on-site Project Manager.

At first Betty was shocked, and then she began to think why not? There was nothing holding her in Albany. The condo sale had not gone well, but she had settled with Peter in his urgency to relocate, and then sold it privately to a co-worker at a higher than asking price, as another buyer was equally interested. The new owner had even purchased most of her remaining furnishings, leaving the limited items to be stored, in her parent's basement. Betty had yet to find a new place so rather than just purchase something for the sake of moving out of her parent's house, she had taken Julia's advice to wait for something she would love to go home to every day. The market was tight right now, but come spring, the market would have more listings and choices.

She was not looking forward to spending the next half a year or more living in her parent's home, leaving a clear decision to accept the offer of Florida. Betty broke the news to her parents on the evening of accepting the offer, ensuring them she would be home for both Thanksgiving and then again for Christmas. These dates were pre-negotiated by all the members of the team, so the client had no choice but to accept. Julia was looking forward to the opportunity of an inexpensive beach holiday and was happily making plans for the first visit home as the two holiday outfits were sifted out while going through Betty's wardrobe for packing. All summer clothing and light sweaters and jackets in one pile went to Florida. No heavy coats, boots, scarves, gloves and woollen hats required, they were moved to the second pile that stayed in Albany.

The Flow-Soft firm secured furnished apartments for the team, pairing up members as requested or discussed for the best possible personality fits. But in the case of Betty, the only other team member that was female was Kim Barkley. Kim, a Database Administrator, had worked on the new release as part of Betty's team. Her work on the project had been accurate and on time, but they only knew each other from the office. Betty understood that assignment completely, and figured the project was expected to be 7 months, with an extra 2 months in the plan for contingency. After living in her parent's home, a roommate, regardless of how difficult, could not be any worse.

The apartment assigned to Betty and Kim was not only a 2 bedroom, 2 bath, but was designed as 2 separate master bedrooms with an attached bath on opposite sides of the unit. The living room, dining area and kitchen were located in the centre of the unit, as was the entry, storage and laundry. The furnishings and décor were all top of the line, including, the leather seating in the living room. The wall colours and accessories were of light-blue shades to bring out the sunshine and beach theme all around the unit. Betty was more than satisfied that the arrangements did not require a coin toss to determine sleeping arrangements and thrilled to see the kitchen was fully equipped with every current cooking accessory.

Even with the apartment rental coverage, the company provided a standard out of town living allowance. That could have covered having all meals in restaurants or takeout, as her roommate Kim preferred. But Betty was happy to shop at the local grocer and take advantage of the fresh produce. Her interest in cooking allowed for an easy transition of her team joining the office by the continual sharing of Latin influenced recipes around the office.

Betty preferred the routine and relaxation that preparing breakfast and dinner provided her on busy workdays. Taking lunch to work had been a necessity of cost saving in university, but it continued into the work schedule as a support of time management. Taking the time at lunch to find a food vendor that would not have her feeling ill for the remainder of the day was too frustrating. Plus, when she considered the expense for what you received at food trucks or takeout options, was a cost cut of both monetary and calories Betty could never completely justify on a regular basis.

However, Kim was the opposite. Kim was petite in build and blonde in hair colour. Betty was not sure if the hair was truly blonde or the monthly efforts of a skilled hair salon. While Betty was happy to shop for groceries on the walk home from work, Kim was planning a night out. Kim would rise late each morning and have a cup of coffee at her office workstation for breakfast. Kim was the office social butterfly and always had a following for lunch out each day. Within the 1st month of being in Miami, Kim had adopted the full beach babe persona.

Her skin had been fully tanned to the perfect golden hue prior to leaving Albany. Not a deep dark tan, just the perfect bronzed colour for her blonde hair to stand out. Kim worked out religiously in the company gym following work each day to retain her trim figure, thus allowing herself a reserve bank of calories that allowed for multiple cocktails in the evenings. Every penny of her pay and living allowance was spent on designer clothing, shoes, purses, and of course the salon.

While Betty was all business, Kim was anything but. Kim went out for lunch every day, out to a club every evening and was always complaining that she was short of money. But the spending and socialising paid off by the second month as Kim had a friend following both at and outside of work and there was one guy who continued to show up in the evenings. He was the complete Miami man. Rock star blond hair that just brushed his shoulder, fit (or 6 pack ripped as Kim informed Betty) and tanned from sailing and beach volleyball. There was clearly money involved as Cameron was always impeccably dressed in, light weight Miami style linen suits, no tie, Italian loafers with no socks and a fancy model of a sports car in a dazzling silver sheen.

In the beginning, Betty was concerned that Kim would bring guys home, so made a habit of leaving the lights and TV on when going to bed hoping that Kim would think she was still up. Betty never really knew if that actually worked because to date Kim had never brought anyone home. Betty never even stayed up to know if Kim came home or when she did. The layout of the apartment allowed for Kim to quietly slip in. But Kim had picked up on the signal and always turned the TV off when she did come home, allowing for a second signal should Kim need a wrap on her door to ensure getting up for work.

When Kim was home, she was very neat and organised eliminating issues for the roommates. The apartment rental included a weekly cleaning service which Kim fully exploited. Her laundry was pre-sorted into baskets with care instructions, dry-cleaning service drop and collect was scheduled for 'maid' day. Betty preferred to do her own laundry. Most of her wardrobe was wash and hang to dry and not having much of a social life left plenty of time for that small chore, plus Betty was not comfortable having someone other than her mother laundering her intimates.

Every week Betty left an envelope address to 'Jamel' with some cash and a thank-you note on her bedside table and every week, Betty's bedding and towels were changed with care. Kim could never remember Jamel's name and was always saying she had to remake her bed regardless of the instructions left.

Chapter 3
Present Day...

Now in Florida, Betty was happy to be away from her parent's efforts to take care of her, and her friends constantly wanting to set her up with another friend. Even casual suggestions of 'just meet him for coffee' were too much and too soon. Now she had Kim as a roommate and while living with Kim was ok, because for the most part Kim was never home, it was Kim not preforming at work that was beginning to weigh on Betty.

Betty took pride in her work, having organisation and ethics at the top of her list. She worked extra hours to ensure a successful software implementation. MDP and Flow-Soft management back in Albany were fully aware of Kim's performance, or lack thereof. Apparently, to date, Kim had covered her mediocre skills by having work friends that covered for her mistakes. Apparently, there was a very talented George Stark, back in Albany pinning for Kim to return and resume their clearly one-sided affair. Kim had started out sending most of her work requirements to George, but as stories of Kim's new Miami beau reached the Albany office, George had stopped sending script solutions or answering Kim's email, calls and texts.

Bart Hartley had taken pity on George by assigning him to an out of country assignment realising his skills were far too valuable to lose over a hormone-based error in judgment. Just being called into Bart's office had been enough for George to divulge the entire story and Bart did not have the heart to punish him further than what was obviously a complete heart stomping by Kim. Bart and Betty discussed Kim's performance at length, and with some task reassignment chose not to act immediately. The project was on its original schedule, and Betty wanted to provide Kim the opportunity to step up and show her own talents.

In some ways, Betty was almost looking forward to going home. Even with the monthly weekend visits by Julia and the two holiday trips home, she was missing the constant contact with Julia, her parents, close friends and extended family. Betty loved the wonderful sunshine of Florida, but missed the anticipation of spring after a tough winter. She had left New York during the beauty and colours of the leaves turning in the autumn allowing the escape from snow and cold. The rented condo was very pleasant, but finally Betty was ready to put her own personal touch to a kitchen, bathroom and mostly her bedroom. She truly felt strong enough to move on just as herself.

The work discussions at lunch had confirmed that Kim was stepping up and holding her own with work requirements. The project Go/No Go date had passed with full agreement from both Betty and Jeremy's teams for a Go. Kim's data conversion was testing well and a software Go Live date was less than a week away.

The condo lease was secured for nine months to allow for project contingency and Bart had personally offered Betty the option of staying in Florida until the lease was complete. There would be the basic warranty support as was common with any software installation, and Bart had offered that to Betty. She could remain in Florida for a few months while new projects were reviewed for her reassignment. Betty had commented to Bart that that did not require her full-time attention, and Bart finally had to explain that it was his way of giving her a bonus for the project.

"Think of it as paid vacation. You can invite friends and family down and play tourist at my expense." Bart Hartley was the most generous man Betty had ever encountered and had already sent an invitation email to both Julia and her parents for visits longer than a weekend. With Kim being out of the condo, there would be wonderful space for guests to enjoy a vacation with her.

Betty returned to the office from lunch to find a buzz of discussion everywhere with the staff, rather than just at Kim's workstation. She truly hoped there was not an issue with the software that had popped up over lunch. Her desk was always left in a neat and organised fashion, so an envelope balanced on her keyboard, glaringly stood out. Betty reached into her purse to check her smart phone for a missed notification, but there were no new messages or alerts.

She placed her purse in the bottom drawer of her desk and swivelled in her chair to address her computer screen and the recently placed envelope. It was not the regular office stationery, even though it held the MDP logo. The paper was the quality Betty had only seen used for wedding invitations. It was truly intended for her, as there printed in a lovely calligraphy script was her full name. Elizabeth McDowall.

Ok, it was certainly for her, but as she picked up the envelope and noted the softness of the paper in spite of being a heavy stock, she tried to think of someone in the office getting married. As Betty could think of no one, and certainly no one called her 'Elizabeth,' she found herself carefully breaking the MDP stamped wax seal and peering inside. She half expected a frog to jump out rather than to see a single card inside.

The card, a simple invitation done in the same calligraphy as the envelope, but now the ink was raised from the paper. That was no stock paper run through the company printer invitation, it was well thought out and planned.

Mr David Baffa
invites you to an
evening 'GO' celebration

The address read Miami Beach, and the date… was of that Friday! No wonder the office was in a buzz if everyone got that same invitation. No RSVP required, after all, who would refuse the owner of MDP.

Betty would just play along, appearing to go, and then just not show up. There was always the 'my cab did not show, or 'there was an accident on the freeway' to delay her arrival. She could surely think of something convincing. Besides what do you even wear to party at the home of the Company CEO and Owner? Julia would know what was appropriate, and Jeremy's wife Susan would know where to find it.

If I make the commitment to a dress, then everyone would think I am going. I can always select a dress suitable for a summer wedding in Albany. The dress would not go to waste.

Company parties were the worst. Even the staff Christmas party prior to going home had been barely avoided, for a date set up, plus the continuous fending off, of drunken advances was not a scene she ever wished to repeat.

After a few phone calls and a date for dinner and shopping with Susan Marlin, Betty was feeling better about the party. Still wanting to bail on the party she met with Susan and it was like the woman could read minds.

"I love spending time with you, and an opportunity to shop is never missed, but I do not understand why you need to buy a dress if you have no intention of attending the party." Susan was settling the dinner bill, before continuing towards the few shops they had selected.

Betty could hardly even respond. Even her own mother was not that quick to pick up on her thoughts, in fact, had never picked up on thoughts at all. "Seriously! How did you ever figure that out?"

Susan just gave a knowing wink and smile. "You forget that I was a very crafty teenager, and then was blessed to have two of my own. I have never had to watch someone work this hard at trying not to go to a party. I am more used to working with opposite reaction to an invitation, or in my case as a teenager, how to get the invitation."

"I appreciate what Mr Baffa is trying to do for everyone. I am just not interested in socialising." Betty was trying to sound convincing.

But Susan was not even remotely in the mood to purchase that less than convincing excuse. "It was all Jeremy and I could do to make you attend the Christmas party. I just don't get how someone so young and pretty does not want to be out in the Miami night life?"

"I have never been a party girl. Plus, it is hard when you do not have an escort." Betty was trying to make her point.

"Is it a date you need? Because I am sure that there is more than one young man at MDP that would be thrilled to fill that role." Susan was sure Jeremy would have at least five names without even having to think hard. She and Jeremy had talked endlessly about men wanting to date Betty.

"I do not want a date, and certainly not one from MDP." That was one item that Betty did not even have to think twice about. Dating within the workplace was a huge line she would never cross.

"Ok, that is fair, actually both Jeremy and I have always respected your ethics to keep romances and affairs out of the workplace." Susan truly respected this in Betty. "How about another date, someone that our girls know?"

"I really appreciate the thought, but I am not ready to date just yet." Not even close Betty thought to herself.

"I understand that, but how about attending with Jeremy and I? We can pick you up, then you are not showing up on your own or having to awkwardly mingle." Susan was hoping that was an agreeable compromise.

"Not a bad idea." Betty was thinking that could actually work. "I would really appreciate that."

"Great! Now let's both find a wonderful dress so Jeremy is not tempted to wander away from us." Susan was pleased that Betty had changed her mind.

"Agreed, but can we look for 2 dresses? I have a feeling that if Mr Baffa is willing to throw such a great 'Go' party, there will also be a project close out celebration." Betty was not interested in having to shop twice in less than a month.

"My girl, I need to make a shopper of you! I have never encountered a female so reluctant to try on clothing. Shopping is a female event. It is even considered a rite of passage in some cultures, especially Miami. My mother could not keep me out of stores, and my daughters make me look like an amateur. Was your mum not a shopper?" Susan was still puzzled after knowing Betty for almost half a year.

"I never really gave it much thought before, but now that you mention it, Mum only shopped when she had a list or an event. I guess I am much the same. Julia and I would go out once a month, and sometimes when she visits here, but even Julia has a list." Betty was beginning to see why she and her roommate Kim were so different. Kim's downtime was either planning to shop or having just returned from shopping.

"Well, you are with an expert now, so let's hit these few shops and find ourselves some beautiful dresses." Susan was now on a mission to have Betty show up looking beyond the successful beauty she was.

The day of the party, Betty sitting at her desk, thinking of the wonderful green silk sheath dress with a matching green sheer chiffon cover that was cut like an overcoat to fall two inches below the hem of the knee length dress. Unlike the solid green of the dress, the jacket had a pattern of a long necked, colourful bird on each of the front panels from the waist down and then followed the same line onto the back panel with a display a vibrant array of long-stemmed flowers.

Betty thought, the artist should have been painting canvas rather than material for dresses, and then thought again, just as well or she would not have such a glorious dress to wear that evening. She and Susan had both purchased simple nude coloured heels and matching evening purse to complete the ensemble. Betty was planning to wear a simple rope of gold necklace and the diamond stud earrings her parents had surprised her with, for her university graduation.

Jeremy broke into her dream when he entered her office with a look of panic. "Betty, so sorry to do this to you, but can you take the 11:00 meeting?"

"Sure, what's wrong?" The party is tonight, we do not need this project to go sideways now!

"Susan just called. She was in a bit of an accident and claims not to be hurt, but I prefer to see for myself." Susan rarely called him at work, so if just a minor dent in the car, she would wait until he got home from work.

"Of course, you need to go! I will handle things here. Call me when you can." Betty was also concerned for Susan.

"I will." Jeremy shouted as he left her office.

Betty was pulling up the meeting agenda when Kim poked her head in the office door. "I heard Jeremy say that Susan was in an accident. Is everything ok?"

"Susan says she is fine, but Jeremy wanted to see for himself. Are you ready for the meeting? I read, you are on the agenda to present an update of the data transfer." Betty was not interested in Kim's need for office gossip.

"Yes, I am ready." Kim was not happy that George was ghosting her messages. She had no intention of returning to winters in Albany. If Cameron did not come through with a proposal for her to stay in Miami, she would need to be assigned to another project implementation, preferably remaining in the southern states.

On the way to the meeting, Kim asked. "Is Jeremy still going to be able to pick you up for the party? Because you know that Cameron and I would be more than happy to give you a lift."

"I had not even thought of a ride to the party. I just want Susan to be fine, and hope only the car needs a repair. I can take a cab to the party, no need for you and Cameron to worry about me." Good grief, who cares about the party. Betty could not believe this was all Kim thought about.

Jeremy called late in the afternoon. Susan was fine but they would be late to the party as the accident had caused a delay for her hair and other appointments. They both suggested, she should go early to socialise in Jeremy's place until they arrived. There were a few last-minute details at the office, so when Betty walked in the door of the condo, she was surprised to see Cameron sitting on the couch in her living room.

"Well, hey there Betty! Kim is just putting on the touches of beauty. She said you need a ride to the party. I am happy to give you a lift. It's a beautiful evening to have the top down." Cameron was acting unusually chatty.

In the months, Cameron had been seeing Kim, he rarely even spoke or acknowledged her presence. Now he was waiting for Kim. Again, something new. Kim was always expected to be ready when he arrived. "Thanks so much Cameron, but I am fine taking a cab. Plus, you will be ready to go shortly and I just walked in the door."

Just as Betty finished her reply, Kim came out looking like something from a fashion magazine. Her dress was slinky and very short. The strappy sandals had to be at least a 5-inch heel. Her blond hair and makeup were done to perfection. Betty had no idea how Kim did this not once, but generally twice a day, she accomplished this with the skill of a professional stylist.

"Betty, you go get ready. Cameron and I will wait. No need for you to take a cab when there is plenty of room in the car." Kim had mentioned giving Betty a ride and Cameron had immediately been in full agreement.

"Kim tells me you do not have a date. I can give one of my friends a call if you would rather have your own escort." Cameron was showing off his perfect white teeth in a forced smile.

"Thank you again, Cameron, but I do not need a date!" Perhaps a little too forceful Betty realised as soon as it was out of her mouth.

"Well, you will just ride with us. Go ahead and get ready we will wait." Kim was not interested in being late and miss one minute of the party, but Cameron had said before Betty got home that they should wait.

"You do not have to wait. Go ahead and get started on the free drinks. I will be there when I can." Betty was hoping that she could use the excuse of not being able to get a cab and just stay home for the evening.

"No, no, you go get ready. Kim and I can put on some music while you get ready. Kim, do you have any Perrier water to sip while we wait?" Cameron was clearly not taking no for an answer.

"Ok, I will get ready. Give me half an hour for a quick shower and change." Entering her room resigned to go to this silly party, Betty was thankful to avoid the set up with one of Cameron's friends. Betty looked out her bedroom window and addressed the cloudless sky and saw Cameron's car. "Oh goody! I get to go to a party with Ken and Barbie and sit in the back seat of Ken's convertible with the top down just like Skipper. Having my hair blown to shit by the time we arrive. Well, Skipper will just have to wear her hair in a ponytail and pray there is scarf that matches the dress to be an accessory following the wind storm."

Betty tried to hide at the party after surviving the arrival with Cameron and Kim. Luckily her ride escorts were more interested in drinks and who was at the party to worry about Betty any longer. That was just fine with Betty. It gave her the opportunity to hide from the crowd and enjoy the lovely old Spanish style two-storey house. Not the contemporary glass and squares seen driving down the road when arriving. There were wood accents and beams in the ceilings to accentuate the white walls, both inside and out.

The floors were mainly polished terrazzo tiles, with the exception of being an inlaid ceramic design in what appeared to be a TV room. Or at least she thought it would be a TV room from the massive TV screen displaying current dance videos and pumped music throughout the main floor. Boy, would her dad love watching football on that screen!

The entry had displayed a wonderful curved staircase that continued to a curved balcony for the upper level. The banister and matching railing were a simple thin twisted wrought iron design that showed class without being flashy. She had yet to meander up the dreamy staircase as the entry was rather busy when she walked in. Even with the spacious rooms and high ceilings the house was loud with music and chatter. There were so many people that any seats available were taken. Even going outside into the courtyard, it was crowded and noisy. The wonderful outdoor kitchen was serving skewers of fruit, vegetables and shrimp.

The inside kitchen could be seen through the lovely glass doors, but was off limits to the guests as the catering firm was not interested in having looky-loos under foot. Just peering in, Betty could see the white cabinets and grey marble countertops. The stove appeared to be a lovely gas range generally found in a restaurant, and the fridge that was continuously being opened could hold food stores for a family of 8 for a month. What a lovely room to have family breakfasts; cooking pancakes to serve up to waiting plates while crazy conversations over the upcoming day's events were discussed, debated and documented to the calendar. It was then that Betty wished for a family of her own that, needed to be fed and organised before heading out in the morning.

A tour around the pool deck was just uncomfortable as it was mainly couples in private moments causing Betty to feel like an intruder. Trying to be social she stopped at various groups where she saw office people, but that seemed to be more of a couple's club crowd and not one that Betty fit into, or even wanted to fit into. She slipped back inside the house through one of the many open balcony doors and was greeted by a server offering a fresh glass of wine.

Seeing Jeremy and his wife, Susan, she accepted a fresh glass and wandered over for a quick hello. Susan was not only the love of Jeremy's life, but a lovely lady and a wonderful mother. When Betty arrived in Miami, she had so many questions about shops and places to go at the office, that Jeremy had extracted himself as the middleman after the first week by inviting Betty to a family BBQ so Susan could answer the questions directly. Susan had immediately accepted Betty as another daughter and was thrilled to have a new, even somewhat reluctant, salon and shopping companion.

"This house is wonderful! Too big and fancy for me, but still a home as well as a showpiece. Susan, you look wonderful, obviously the accident today was not serious." Betty inserted herself into Jeremy and Susan's discussion of the outdoor pool.

"Oh Betty, so lovely to see you here. Jeremy and I were hoping you would come and not stay back in your condo on a Friday night." Susan's smile was genuine, and the comment was something her own mum would have said. "I am sorry to have given everyone a scare today and caused Jeremy to rush home." She squeezed Jeremy's arm and leaned into him to kiss his cheek.

"Did you take a cab? Sorry we were running late and did not pick you up." Jeremy was always concerned about her.

"No cab, I was able to catch a ride with Kim and her boyfriend. You had Susan to worry about, so no need to apologise." Betty was fine to not get into the details of Cameron suggesting a date as well as a ride.

"Well, you look lovely, so very happy to see you out. Now we just have to find someone to take you out more often." Susan and Jeremy were both anxious to see Betty in a happy relationship.

"It would not go well with Mr Hartley if I missed this party. Celebrating the project Go with this affair leads me to wonder what will be the venue when we actually go live?" Betty hated to think of another party, but was glad she and Susan had been able to acquire two outfits each, on their last shopping trip.

"I am happy you came, as will Bart, but really Betty, you need to get out more. You are much too young to be all work and no play. If you keep this pace going, you will never allow the opportunity to meet someone, and heaven forbid you end up with my work schedule." Jeremy was just being kind. Accurate, but kind and caring.

"There is no chance of Betty ever ending up like you Jeremy. For one thing, she is far too pretty and kind to be held behind a desk the way you are my dear." Susan gave Betty a wink and her husband an intimate shoulder rub.

How could she get out of this thread of conversation? Betty thought.

"Say have you even seen our host? I have been wandering around the house and have no clue what he even looks like to introduce myself and offer my thanks for the invitation."

"He was here just before we saw you, so he could not have gone far. Easy to spot, young, handsome, wealthy, just the man you need to meet." Jeremy was teasing, but Betty was still not interested.

Betty figured Jeremy was exaggerating as how could a person have built such a successful pipeline company like MDP and amassed so much wealth and still be anywhere close to her age. She would use the excuse of seeking out this mysterious Mr Baffa herself to extract herself from any possible set up introductions by Jeremy and Susan. "Have you seen the staircase at the front of the house?"

"Oh yes!" Susan replied and then continued to provide a detailed description. "We went up first thing when we arrived. I asked one of the greeters if it was allowed and he said yes, but the upper rooms were off limits. So up we went and then stood on the balcony at the top of the stairs watching other guests arrive. It started to get busy so we continued on. You need to go up yourself. The stained-glass dome in the ceiling is spectacular even at night, I would love to come back and see it again with the sunlight beaming through."

"Well, that sounds like where I need to head next and then scout out our generous host." With that parting comment, Betty headed out into a hallway and appeared to be in search of the path to the staircase.

But instead of the staircase, Betty began scouting the hallway for a guest powder room. In a house this size, there had to be at least one on this level. Even if she had to ask and then wait in a queue. It would give her a plausible hiding spot for another possible hour, and then just casually slip out the front door. She could easily grab one of the continuous cabs dropping people off, to get back home unnoticed. Kim would not even be looking for her much less care.

The hallway was dimly lit and Betty was thinking that was to help direct people into the areas of the house where the host would like people to stay. Made sense to Betty, but because the hallway was not totally dark, or closed off, it was not off bounds. Seeing some of the wait staff scooting in and out of the kitchen to replenish trays or make the rounds with freshly loaded trays she thought that may be a good place to look for a washroom or a quiet way to exit the house.

There was one closed door that was locked when she tested the door handle. I could stand there and wait for the next server to scoot by and ask if that truly was a washroom, she thought to herself. She leaned against the wall, thinking that the new pumps were more comfortable than expected. Maybe she would have to go look for other colours in that same brand for work.

She turned her head to note the presence of another person entering the hallway. Not entirely strange that, that man was a bit wobbly, but not really in the mood to deal with a drunk, she reached for her bag to extract her phone. Maybe if she appeared to be texting or calling someone, the guy would not engage.

He continued towards her and did not appear to notice her as he took a key from his pants pocket to open the locked door. Good grief! The guy was so hammered that he could not even get the key in the lock. I was going to stay there and continue to be invisible. There was no need for me to get involved and that was obviously not the washroom, so let's move down the hall and see what I can find. If that guy had the keys to the house and was drunk, Mr Baffa was not going to be very impressed. That guy deserved to be fired for getting drunk at a home he was obviously employed at. Deserved it! Of course, he did…

Shit! "Can I help you with that lock?" Betty turned back the few steps she had taken away and reached out towards his hand to steady the key.

The guy relaxed his hand at her touch and leaned his forehead against the still closed door. Betty took the key and inserted it into the lock with a turn, and heard the click of release, but before she could turn the knob, she placed a hand up on the man's shoulder to make him aware of her presence. "You need to not be leaning against this door when I open it."

He barely lifted his head and murmured a very weak "thanks."

Betty turned the handle and the door swung inward to reveal a small landing and flight of stairs to the second level of the house.

The man stumbled forward and gripped the handrail and moved about three steps before he stumbled forward. Betty rushed forward to be at his level on the stairs and held him by the waist. "Come on big guy. Let's get you up these stairs and out of the sight of your boss."

She helped him up a set of stairs that were designed to be used by the staff. Their progress was slow and it was not only his breathing that was laboured by the time they reached the 2nd floor landing. There was another door at the top of the stairs, but it had no lock from the inside so, Betty reached forward opening a door to a wonderful laundry room. WOW! Her mum would be in seventh heaven with this!

His moans brought her attention back into focus. "Damn these automatic lights." As he shielded his eyes. "That door on the left." He pointed, just as Betty saw in the light there was a grey tinge to his beautiful bronze skin.

The door on the left opened to a brilliant white marble bathroom. The windows were letting in light from the pool area allowing ease of vision without adding more. "No lights on I am guessing?" Betty quietly questioned the man she was supporting. He nodded in agreement and wanted to lie down on the floor. Betty helped him lower on the floor and held the back of his head as the relief of no longer having to stand caused him to go completely slack. The last thing she needed was for him to bounce his head on that marble, adding a concussion to his already weakened state.

He murmured a quiet thanks for not letting his head bash, and felt her hand gently sliding away to be replaced by something soft as Betty shoved a towel, she had pulled from the nearby rack under his head.

"Ok, not sure who you are, but you obviously know this house. What is wrong with you? Too much to drink?" Betty was not interested in playing nursemaid to some puking drunk.

"I'm David." He was struggling to talk now. "I ate something, not sure if an allergic reaction or someone is trying to poison me."

"*The David*?" Betty was stunned. "Shit! Sorry, of course you are." No wonder he knew the house and had a key. What the hell? "Why would someone want to poison you? I need to call for help and 911." Betty began to reach into her purse for her phone.

He grabbed her hand to stop the phone call. "No police, no ambulance."

Chapter 4

"Why the hell not? This is serious! If someone is trying to hurt you, don't you think the police need to be involved?" Betty had never spoken directly to a police officer, but that did not diminish her regard.

His hands moved to her shoulders and he pulled her closer. "I can trust no one but you right now. Please help me!" The begging look from his soft brown eyes was better than any puppy at a shelter.

"Shit! Sorry! I don't ever use foul language, but this is really bizarre and stressful for me." Betty could hardly think. What to do? How to help him? "I am no doctor! You need a doctor, real medical help!"

"Please, no doctors and definitely no police!" David was panicked enough by the threat of her calling the police that his grip tightened on her shoulders. "I have things here that you can use."

"Ok, I am not going to leave you or call the police, even though I still think that is the right thing to do." She reached for his hand to relieve the pressure on her own shoulder, even sick the guy was still strong! "I am no doctor but I have first aid training that has been kept current since high school, but that hardly qualifies me to deal with poisoning!"

David could hear the frantic tinge in her voice and knew she was likely his best hope for help also knew he needed to stay both engaged and conscious. "There are first aid supplies in that vanity." He pointed to the larger of the two sinks that were basically bare.

"Do you not have a wife or partner that I need to go and find? She should be helping you." Betty was still working for the exit angle.

"There is only you. I live here mostly alone, staff of course, but no wife or partner." David cringed at a new stomach cramp.

"Ok, let's first define what this may be." Betty needed to move into an organised mode as she resigned herself to be the important man's nursemaid. "What have you eaten or drank this evening?"

With a bit of a shaky voice, David began to recall and told her that he could remember. "I had a soda water with lime, which has not been refreshed since guests began to arrive. I am not much of a drinker, so having something in my hand when people arrive lets them form their own opinion and releases me from having to chat too much. I can then just send them to the bar for their own drink while I continue to greet others." David was thankful, she was engaging in a solution rather than trying to bolt.

"So that eliminates drinks, how about food or a snack?" Betty formed a list in her mind.

"They were grilling pineapple at the outdoor kitchen. My one great weakness." He admitted, with a look that reminded Betty of a boy caught with his hand in a cookie jar. "I stood chatting to a young couple while a new batch was coming off the grill. I only had one slice." He still looked ashamed of his indulgence.

"I hardly think that a slice of grilled pineapple is going to take any diet over the edge." She was primarily trying to alleviate the guilt factor. And then moved to research. "Have you eaten pineapple before?"

"Oh plenty, as I said before a great weakness." He still looked guilty.

"So not a new food, but if you prepared your own first drink, and no one else at the party is ill, or obviously there would be a commotion or some indication…" Betty grabbed her phone again. "There has to be something being put on the pineapple between the time of coming off the grill and you eating."

David closed his eyes to think about the pineapple. "I was talking to a young couple while waiting. They were waiting as well." David paused trying to picture what they looked like. "Then the man said to his wife that she should sit down at a nearby table so her feet would not hurt in her new shoes and that he would bring us all a slice when it was done."

"Sounds like a thoughtful guy, not that I have ever dated anyone that cared if my shoes hurt my feet." Betty was a little envious of this girl.

"Yeah, don't really understand why women insist on wearing shoes that hurt them." David thought of his own mother, but she was never one to wait to be told to take a seat, she would have given the order to his father to wait for the slices and bring them to her. That would have been done very lovingly, but still on her terms.

Betty noted the little smile on his face and wondered if the man had no respect for women and their needs. "Well, most of us are so busy trying to look good for men, we endure much more than just sore feet."

"I am sorry, I cannot afford to annoy the one person caring for me. I was just thinking of my own mother and the silly shoes she always wears for the sake of fashion." David did not need his Florence Nightingale to stomp away pissed-off, leaving him to die over shoes. "I am putting all of my trust in a stranger, I do not even know your name. But you do wear lovely shoes." He clearly noted the removal of shoes to show lovely slender feet with just a light-pink polish on the nails.

Betty relaxed and thought of her own mother and the silly shoes she would wear for formal events. "I like nice shoes but will not subject myself to anything that is not comfortable." So there! But both of them look at her feet and removed shoes. "My name is Betty, and I only removed my shoes so it is easier to move around." Betty tried to get in the last word on the subject of shoes.

"Am I to take it that this last comment was not just about shoes? Betty, I have no intention of putting you in a situation with the police. But I really do need your help!" David was prepared to even offer this woman money, but so far that had not come up. Interesting…

"Point taken, but if this goes sideways, I will be calling 911. Just want to be clear that I will not be responsible for someone dying!" That was rather forceful, and unnecessarily on the bitchy side. Betty, stop that!

"Agreed. If my heart stops you can call 911 and be clear of any responsibility. But so far, I am feeling weak and sick, not having my life flash before my eyes and wanting a Priest." At least not yet, David thought.

"Ok, back on track, did you stay at the grill with the man, or go with the woman?" Betty had her phone open on an internet search window and was starting to type in pineapple reactions.

"My manners got the best of me, and I escorted the woman to a table next to the grill. We had barely seated ourselves when the young man set down the plates of slices." David thought of the engagement, recalling helped him avoid slipping into that lulling comfort of sleep that was inviting his mind.

"You turned your back on this man getting your food, and if it was up that quickly, why the need for the woman to sit down so urgently?" Betty stopped her search of pineapple and replaced the search with poison symptoms. "He put something on your pineapple!" She shouted to herself while typing.

Betty's shout startled David, but it also spurred the clarity of the memory. "He did not just bring a plate of slices, he had three separate plates and put them down very deliberately. 'This is yours my dear. This is yours sir. Let's dig in!' He had napkins and ensured they stayed until I had eaten mine. He did not even touch his own." The memory was becoming clearer. "He served her first, as that one was clear, but could not risk a mix up on the other two so doctored them both."

"He never ate his and when I was done, he grabbed the woman's hand and named someone they had to go and say hello to, before he lost sight of the person. They almost bolted from the table. Someone else immediately sat down and introduced themselves and we talked a bit until I started to feel ill and excused myself. I knew I needed to get upstairs to this bathroom. And you were the angel that got me here. I am in your debt." This time when David reached for Betty's shoulder it was not to grip her but instead to endearingly hold.

"Well doctoring your pineapple was certainly a great term, he wanted you to call a doctor. That was a rather well-planned setup by the sound of things. I wonder if the second couple were also part of the ruse." Betty was focused on her phone search, but noted that the hand on her shoulder was not leaving. Maybe he needed to retain that contact that sick people often did, for comfort. He was not being inappropriate by any stretch of the imagination, so Betty let his hand linger there, as the connection of warmth was soothing her nerves.

Once the browser on her phone had revealed a worthy link, Betty clicked it open and was ready to define the poison source. "We know you were likely poisoned as you thought, so let's move to define what that poison is. I have just opened a list that allows you to check off symptoms that can help identify what the poison may be. Do you have a headache?"

They moved through the list one item at a time. Betty did not want him to just answer fast, leading to possibly missing a critical item. She was far too logical and disciplined in her work to allow a mistake. The same detail, if not more, was required now.

While it only took 5 minutes, to David it felt like hours. Finally, Betty stopped with the questions and just read. "So, what do I have doc?" He was trying to lighten the severity of the situation.

Betty looked up from the phone at him, and then smiled. "Well, the bad news is that you are going to die, but the good news is that it will not be today, if I can help it." She had humour as well. Yes, she did!

David liked this retort. "Give it to me straight doc."

"Once more to clarify, I am not a doctor but this is what I am thinking it is, Jimsonweed." Betty said the word with relief.

"What the hell is Jimsonweed? Sorry for the foul language, but I have never heard of this." David was trying to think.

"No apology required. I have never heard of it either. Apparently, it can display itself in several areas of the body particularly; the digestive system, nervous system, vascular system and urinary system. You have many of the symptoms but most importantly they continually recommend seeking professional medical treatment. Are you sure you do not want to go to a hospital?" Reading the reality of this situation and performing first aid were far apart from the written recommendations. Betty was less comfortable with each site she reviewed.

"Absolutely no hospital! I need this kept very quiet. Please, you have helped me this far, can you please stay with me?" David was at the point of begging in his voice.

Betty was not immune to such a desperate plea for assistance, she was just not at all comfortable being responsible for such a critical health issue. "Ok, under one condition, and this I need to be very clear on. If you become unresponsive or go into cardiac arrest, I will be calling 911."

"Agreed." David conceded. It was clear she was not comfortable but was completely trustworthy. "I am thinking that all the medical supplies that we need should be in that cabinet." David pointed again to the larger of the vanities.

Betty moved around David to open the cabinet and began to take out items as per the inventory list of possible medical treatments a patient could expect to receive. Not that she knew how to use any of that stuff. As the items were laid out on the floor, Betty was thrilled to see that each package contained a well-written list of instructions. "Apparently, documentation is not just limited to software applications."

"What?" David was focused watching her assemble items, while she checked her phone.

"Documentation is what I ensure is thoroughly prepared for each software implementation we complete. The training team cannot stay with the client forever. They need to be capable and comfortable with the software I implement, so we leave detailed guides of instruction for different task roles as well as an overall user guide of the general application. Apparently, whoever left all of this equipment gets complete credit and thanks, for the detailed instructions in each package." Betty continued to read each item laid out on the floor.

"The first thing is not to induce vomiting, but it is also imperative that you consume large amounts of fluids. If the forcing of liquids is not effective, we may need to use the active charcoal as a last resort." Opening another cabinet, Betty was thrilled to see a full case of bottled water. Reaching in to pull out the whole case, there was a thud when it hit the marble floor causing David to jump in alarm.

"Was that someone trying to break into my room?" David had zoned out and after the thump was trying to sit up unsuccessfully.

Betty moved back to him and rested a hand on his shoulder. "No, I am so sorry to startle you. That was me, hauling out the case of water. You need to drink a lot of this, to help your body metabolise the drug."

"I am not sure what I can drink but I will try. But first, can you please lock that door." David pointed to the door from the laundry room which they had entered. "And then please go through that door to ensure the bedroom door is also locked." This time as David moved to point to the opposite door, the arm was much lower indicating his weakened state.

Betty rose and secured the lock to the laundry room. Then gingerly stepped over David to move through the door into the bedroom. The bedroom was enormous with a king size bed, hardly looking like more than a child's cot in the large space. There was a cosy sofa set in front of a fireplace with a fuzzy rug between the two pieces. Once the bedroom door lock was secured, Betty stopped at the sofa to grab two chenille pillows and a throw. Returning to the bath, she left the door to the bedroom half-open, so they could be made aware of any attempts to enter the bedroom.

David nodded at Betty for leaving the door in a half-open state, and in her absence had moved himself against the cool marble side of the tub. Betty assisted him to sit in the partial sit up pose, with the help of pillows and towels. He was too warm for the throw right now, but that could quickly change should a fever appear.

"Ok, let's try to get some of this water into you." Betty unscrewed the cap on the first bottle and held the bottle while David began to drink. As his sips moved towards greedy gulps Betty pulled the bottle away. "Thirst is a symptom, but you just have to take sips and ensure each one is swallowed. We do not need you choking."

David nodded his agreement and re-took the bottle to only sip the water.

By the time the first bottle was consumed and Betty was opening a second, she noticed that his breathing was fast and shallow. "You have to try and focus on taking deep breaths. I know this is hard when trying to drink so how about you take a deep breath then a sip. If you cannot breathe deep, it will mean you may need support breathing and that is one medical treatment that will require a professional."

"With all of this water, it will be good to be in the bathroom." David was trying to bring some light into their serious situation. She was counting to 5 while he breathed in and then counted again while he exhaled.

"In, 2-3-4-5 and out for 5. Urine production is very critical for your care. That will be very important to monitor." Betty was happy the breathing was going well as was the nearly empty second bottle of water.

David saw her reach for a third bottle of water and was not happy with the thought of needing assistance to take a piss. "Ok, now you are dangerously close to moving from a dreamy Florence Nightingale to Nurse Ratchet. You will NOT be monitoring me on a toilet!"

"Well, you were the one that insisted that I stay and take care of you. So, if you cannot get to that toilet on your own, I will not be leaving this room only to come back and find, you have cracked your head open on all this beautiful marble, having fallen off the toilet!" Betty actually smiled at the thought of such an important man needing help to the bathroom. Then the smile faded when she thought this was not funny, but rather sad to be at the mercy of a caregiver for basic needs.

"First you smiled then you took on a look of concern. Is there more on that list of symptoms and care that you have yet to share?" David was not a man to be without control and his self-control was most distressing, even with such a beautiful creature continually kneeling over him.

"If you are not able to process the water your stomach will bloat and then instead of the indignity of me helping you to the toilet to pee, I will be holding your head over the toilet after giving you the activated charcoal packet." Neither was an amusing option in Betty's opinion.

"Drinking water and assistance to the toilet is much preferred to the charcoal. How about you talk while I breathe deeply and slowly drink my water." David felt his head moving from a headache to being rather fuzzy. "I am starting to feel a bit spaced out, so if you talk, it will give me a point of focus."

"Me talk? About what?" Betty thought that maybe, he would be interested in hearing about the software implementation. "I can tell you about the software implementation if you like?"

"I know all about the software implementation and its progress to date and am correct in assuming that you are Betty McDowall in charge of that project?" David had been keeping his thoughts straight by piecing the evening together.

"How do you know my full name? I have never even met you." Betty was shocked and began to feel a little uncomfortable.

"Relax, I put it together. We have not met, but you are at this party and said you were a project manager. You are the only person of that title that would be here so it was a guess that I calculated correctly." David continued to drink and ensured that he was able to breathe deeply.

"Oh, that makes sense, and you are right, I am your project manager. Can we talk about this lovely house?" Betty was looking for another topic.

"I know all about this house however, I know nothing about *Betty*. Who is she, and more importantly, why is she at this party alone?" David remembered being pleased when he heard that she was all business and not interested in the office dating game nor the Miami club scene.

Betty began a rather vanilla flavoured bio of herself. Her home in Albany, university credentials, business acumen but nothing of herself other than to say, she was not currently dating anyone.

David listened and drank his water. He still felt a little fuzzy, but thankfully his stomach was not bloating and he actually thought a trip to the toilet would be required. "I could have read your resume and gotten all of that. But we will hold for a few minutes because I actually need to use the toilet. If you can help me stand, I will see if this is possible on my own."

Betty moved closer to help steady David as he used both her helping hand and the side of the tub to raise himself. Once standing, he took a moment, with his eyes closed to get his balance and then slowly opened to see Betty inches from his nose with the scrutiny of a mother watching a child. He intentionally leaned on the top of her head; she was barely at his shoulder with no shoes on. "I'm ok, you can relax and do some of that deep breathing yourself."

David could feel the breath release from Betty with a sigh of relief. "Can you take a few steps and manage your clothing?" Hoping with everything, that she could excuse herself from the room before any clothing was removed.

David responded by moving away on his own. Using the wall for additional support, he almost laughed. "They are called pants; you can say the word pants and not offend anyone. And yes, I will try this on my own. I promise to call if I am going down."

Betty slipped out into the bedroom and instead of looking around the room she found herself, with her ear to the not fully closed door. She could hear some muffled movements and then the toilet flushing and the tap running. She stepped back into the bathroom uninvited and David looked up from the sink as he washed his hands. "I did it all on my own, even zipped up my pants again. However, I do need to sit down again before I fall down."

"Do you want to try and come into the bedroom and lay down on your bed?" Betty thought the comfort would be greater.

"No, I think the floor may still be the best option as I am not sure about the stomach. The bed would be much too far in a dash." David moved back to the tub. The ledge was rather wide allowing for a good seating space. Rather than lowering himself to the floor as before, Betty moved the towels and pillows to provide some cushion and comfort as he settled in with his back to the wall. Betty lifted his legs up onto the ledge, wanting to maintain an even blood flow and then opened his fourth bottle of water.

"Do you feel nauseous?" Betty sat on the other end of the tub ledge and unlocked her phone screen to again review the symptoms and treatment.

"More dizzy and foggy than nauseous now that I am sitting down." David was actually relieved to be sitting again. Standing-up had taken much more energy than he would have ever imagined. "You are not off the hook, back to you and no more resume items. How are you so lovely and single in Miami?"

Betty blushed at the comment of being lovely. She never considered herself beautiful, and had been called cute by a boy in high school, but even Peter had never called her lovely or pretty. "I was in a long-term relationship that ended just before coming to Miami and am not interested in the dating scene."

Even in his fuzzy state, David noted the blush. Had no one ever told her how beautiful she was? "Just how long was this relationship that ended? Were you married?"

"Not married. We were living together for 5 years after university, and over dinner one evening, he announced that he was not ready to marry, so felt it best to end things." Betty was just sticking to the facts.

"Still the facts, Betty. Good that he was man enough to tell you that, but it took him 5 years to come to that conclusion? Seems rather false to me." David felt she was much better without this guy.

"It was more than false; you are right on the mark there, Mr Baffa. Less than 2 months after moving out, he sent me a letter through his lawyer, that I needed to sell the condo we owned jointly as he was getting married and moving to Manhattan." Betty flushed even deeper with the emotion of recalling the sting of receiving that blunt letter.

"No Mr Baffa please, only David. After spending time together in my bathroom and with all of my trust in you makes us instant friends." David could not believe this guy. "You owned a condo with this guy, and he sent you a letter through a lawyer to ask for money back? What is wrong with this guy?"

"I would rather say, what was wrong with me. Apparently, he had been involved for some time with the women he was moving to Manhattan with, and I was totally clueless. As to his character, I am putting him in the class of coward." Finally, able to say that out loud about Peter, made her feel much stronger in herself.

"I would say this is totally on him and you were duped. Did his friends know about the affair and not tell you?" David could not believe how she was accepting this as her fault.

"No one knew. They kept it very secret. Peter's friends were just as shocked as I was. They all told me that he was a fool, but in reality, I was the fool." Betty was back to the facts again and David was sensing this.

"I disagree on the fool part. But you sold the condo and gave him back his half of the proceeds without a fight? In most states you would be considered the same as married, so you could have held your ground. I am thinking the state of New York has similar laws." David was appalled that someone would treat a woman this way. She had certainly gotten the coward label correct.

"Honestly, I was not up for the fight. By that point, I was ready to leave the condo and begin to move on. I moved back in with my parents and put the condo on the market." With those final words, David heard a bit of a change in her voice and looked up at her to see a faint smile on her face.

"What is with the smile? It could not be, the having to move back in with your parents!" David loved his mother but the thought of living under the same roof made his delicate stomach flip over.

"My parents are wonderful, caring and very supportive. But moving home was horrible after being away for about 9 years. Not that they were horrible, it was just defeating for me. I was in the process of finding my own place again when the project with your firm came up. So, for that David, I am very thankful." Betty touched his leg to further imply the thanks were genuine.

The touch of her hand felt warm and caused him to note the finely shaped but short nails in the same pink as the toes. Her hand was slender and long in proportion to her size. But David refocused on the dud boyfriend. "Did it take long to sell the condo?" David thought money must have been tight to not purchase another while the sale was active. Most banks would have supported a bridge loan.

"It did take some time and the realtor actually gave up the listing after a month." Betty said with a smirk.

"I do not know a realtor that would give up after a month. There is more to this sale than you are telling." David liked the smirk, much more than the serious face and wondered what a full smile and laugh would do to change her appearance.

"I have never told a soul this. Not even my best friend Julia. So, you can never, ever, tell anyone." Betty was suddenly worried he would think less of her and it would break their trust.

"Well, we are in my bathroom with my own need for secrecy, so I promise I will never tell anyone." To further emphasise his promise he instinctively gave the sign of the cross, so engrained from his Catholic upbringing.

"Are you sure you want me to keep talking. The last thing we need is me to wear you out further." Betty was stalling.

"Please, you are clearly stalling, besides staying focused on your voice is my point of reference." Plus, David wanted to hear the story, and he was very sure there was more to the story.

Betty began her story. "I was so angry for the first few days following the letter from Peter's Lawyer, my friends and co-workers were continuously asking if they had somehow offended me. I decided that all that anger needed to be redirected and quickly, or not only would I be single, but also be alone without friends. So, I replied to the lawyer that the sale of the condo could happen immediately. I moved back home as that was simple and I had no idea where to look or what I could afford. My parents helped me move, but I told my parents that I needed some time to myself before leaving the condo."

Betty got a fresh bottle of water for David and one for herself. Taking a long drink and a very deep breath she continued. "I left the condo with spoiled food in the fridge, in condiment jars with the lids not sealed – looked like the fridge was clean. The garbage can appeared to be empty but under the bag was something rotting. After the listing was active, I went back and blew up an egg in the microwave, that is easy enough to clean with a lemon in water later, but horrible to see or open. Peter thought I was still living there so never went over, and I had asked for his key when he moved out. After the first month, and the only offer was for a third of the asking price, and the realtor told Peter she would not continue." Betty took a break to drink more water.

"Interesting so far, but clearly not the end." David knew there was more. This was one lady who was much more than she appeared.

"No, not the end." With a deep sigh, Betty continued. "The next letter from Peter's lawyer was signing over the condo title to me as it was worth less than the mortgage we held."

"He left you holding the mortgage?" David could not believe this guy!

Betty actually laughed. "He did. The mortgage was for about half of the original asking price so Peter felt that leaving me with that was better than having to pay the bank. Since I knew why it was not selling, I accepted, with the lawyer saying that I would be moving back in rather than selling. Instead, I returned to the condo spent less than one hour with lemon and baking soda, after removing the fouled items and returned the next day, after the windows being left open to find the place not bad."

"I then hired a professional carpet and fabric cleaner to remove any other odours. By the end of that week, I could have moved back as the mortgage payment was manageable but I truly had no desire to live there ever again. All the memories I thought I had of Peter and I, were as sour as the garbage I had removed."

"I placed a formal sale by owner notice in the newspaper, on Facebook and at work and ended up with a bidding war in three days. With the advice of my own lawyer, I told each of the bidders of the mutual interest and asked them to submit a written bid to my lawyer that showed their complete finance information. The bids were then opened by the lawyer and myself one at a time and compared."

"I ended up accepting a cash offer that was 15% more than my asking price, which was only 10,000 dollars less than the original list price, and no realtor costs. The successful buyers, were the parents of a recent graduate, with very few possessions, so they also offered a separate purchase for most of the contents."

"Peter had already taken what he wanted, being the two pieces of art, we had bought together, but I figured that was well worth the price as I got the better deal in the end. I had my personal things and with the extra money could not only start searching for something new, but would be able to furnish it as I wanted as well."

"That was where I was when Bart Hartley offered me the project manager position for the MDP implementation." Betty gave huge sigh of relief with the story finished. It felt strangely good to have finally said it out loud. Julia deserved to hear this as well and Betty vowed to give her a call as soon as she could.

"Well good for you! I seriously underestimated you. Remind me to never evict you." David began to understand the smile and laugh when she started her story, but now wanted to see both again without the slimy Peter involved. "So, I need to try the toilet thing again. That is a good thing, right?"

This time she did smile at him. The smile reached from her lovely mouth through her cheeks and settled into her lovely brown eyes. "It is a very good thing. We will start with standing again before I leave the room."

David noticed the nausea was much less and the fog in his head was still there, but the dizzy feeling when he stood did not happen like last time. She left the bathroom and this time he was aware that her step did not go beyond the reach of the closed bedroom door.

David was never so happy to report on his ability to piss, as he was this second time. He opened the door to his bedroom to find her standing there like a nervous mother. For some strange reason, he found her presence and concern very comforting. "I think I will trade the marble for my bed." David smiled as the previous blush in her cheeks returned.

"Ok, I can grab the pillows and throw and sit on the sofa while you get some rest." Betty was hoping he would ask her to leave, that would be the ultimate end to this crazy night.

A knock sounded on the bedroom door, followed by a male voice questioning his presence, giving both Betty and David a start.

David's response was rather curt. "Give me a break Josh."

The only sound from the other side of the door was a muffled laugh. Betty looked at David with wide eyes. "He thinks I am a girl from the party and we are having sex!"

David laughed. "Yes, my lovely nurse. You will not be settling in on the couch." David pointed to a drawer in highboy. "Grab a big t-shirt and change in the bathroom. I will toss my clothing around and then will need you to do the same. Please leave that wonderful dress as a pool on the floor. I promise to have it professionally cleaned and pressed when this is over."

Chapter 5

At the embarrassment of David beginning to discard his clothing, Betty grabbed the first t-shirt her hand touched when she opened the drawer. She turned back as to make a comment, but found her tongue tied at the sight of David with no shirt. He was lean and toned, complete with a genuine 6 pack for abs! Peter had claimed he had abs of steel, but they certainly never looked this good!

Betty ran for the bathroom. *Coward.* She muttered to herself as she removed her own clothing, brushed out the ponytail of hair and straightened-up the bathroom, to avoid a quick return to the bedroom. Seeing David with no shirt was enough, no need to embarrass herself more by standing with a gaping mouth should she walk in, to find him with even less clothing on.

Bringing the pillows and throw back into the bedroom with her clothing, she began to place items first sensibly at the sofa to replicate their original positioning and then let her mind drift to a wonderful and purely lustful interlude with this very handsome partner. How they could enter the room with an intent and anticipation of being alone. Once the door was shut and locked against intruders, the first intimate embrace and kiss that would spin her head and cause the beginning of stirrings in her lower stomach. This would be a perfect spot for the removal of her sheer jacket and discarding of shoes.

The pool of her dress, she ensured by stepping back into it at the spot David had indicated, and then letting it drop while imagining his hands at her back, lowering the zipper and then him reaching under her shoulders to slide his hands possessively down her arms, allowing the dress to pool at the base of her feet. Feeling rather light headed she dropped her bra, removed in the bathroom, at the base of the bed with a giddy vision of this incredibly fit man lifting her from the silky feel of the carpet to be tossed on the bed with little regard, for the force of her landing.

David had tossed the decorative pillows and top cover onto his side of the floor and was now lying under a sheet that had been pulled from its pristine folded tucks. She expected him to be dozing or asleep by now but took a deep breath of shock to note that he was staring at her. The shock deepened into a rather clear blush of embarrassment when Betty realised that he had been watching her entire performance.

No snide comment, or pithy retort, and not even a sly smile. David simply turned back the sheets on her side of the bed to welcome her to join him. She even noted that there were 2 top sheets, one rather heavy and one of a much lighter fabric designed to allow for comfort, depending on the temperature of the room. David was only covered with the heavier of the sheets and the lighter was bunched against him leaving her the modest protection of a sheet while being held against him.

Betty smiled at the thought and lost her embarrassment momentarily while she lifted her knee up to crawl into the enormous bed. "I appreciate the consideration for this charade, but want to be clear that this is way beyond my normal behaviour."

"I thought you did a wonderful performance with the staging and will envy the fortunate man that is worthy of sharing such an experience in reality with you." David was too weak to think further than the slight imagination of seeing that performance again, staring himself as the male role. "But you did forget one thing."

Betty sat on the edge of the bed and scanned the room. To her mind it was rather brilliant. She turned to David lying rather calmly with his length filling almost the entire space of the long and deep bed. "I don't think so."

David just sighed. "You forgot your panties. Fling them against that wall beside you as that would be my dominant hand."

The blush returned, but not just pink. This time it was a fire-engine red that filled her body, from toes to the top of her head. There was no emotion in his words, simple facts to keep the ruse in play. Betty had to take a deep steadying breath to get her bearings. She felt like being on a cruise ship with her parents and having sat in the sun too long. "Right." Was the only response she could manage, then rose to remove her panties in the least revealing way with the shortness of the t-shirt. The toss was pathetic by any standard, as she plopped her butt back on the mattress.

This time David did smile. Not the expected callous smile she had observed, by men watching a woman in a short skirt, but smile to appreciate the effort that task involved. "Now bring that flushed body over here and warm me as I am starting to shiver with cold."

Betty moved under the sheets, bringing her length against his and noted instantly the shiver was not exaggerated. She reached to his forehead and instead of the chill found the warmth of a low-grade fever. "It is a side effect from the Jimsonweed and am happy to say not a high fever. The chills could be from sitting in the bathroom on the cold marble, so just try to rest and if your fever grows, I will grab a cool cloth for your head. I am hoping that with the water you drank it will wash the drug out naturally. Let me know if you become thirsty again, as water is currently your best medicine."

David only grunted an acknowledgement of her assessment, and proceeded to pull her closer leaving his arms and one leg holding her in place like a soothing body pillow. Within a few minutes, he dozed-off to sleep that she prayed would be healing for his body and mind. Not full of the hallucinogens that she read, could enter someone's psyche.

Betty continued to monitor his fever and was pleased when his entire body temperature stabilised. The slight warmth in his forehead remained, but certainly not a fever and the shiver of chills had ceased within minutes of David's sleeping. His arms and shoulders were not cool to her touch as she ran her fingers along the finely sculpted muscles.

Even in the light, streaming in through the uncovered windows, she noted that his colour was returning. The paleness and slight grey tinge, she had noted under the lights of the laundry room had vanished but he was not clear by any stretch, according to the medical posts reviewed on her phone.

As Betty continued her vigil of monitoring any spike in a fever, she realised that it was not just a tan on his skin, but that he had some Latin background. His English contained no accent, that would indicate Spanish or Italian the two main languages, that came to her mind while considering his darker skin tone.

Betty laid her arm next to his. Even with her visiting the beach on weekends and walking to and from work in the glorious sunshine, the slight colouring change for herself still paled in comparison to this man. Her software firm rented a furnished condo and provided a daily allowance for food and expenses, which would have allowed for a car service and eating out, but Betty was happy to walk to and from work and the limited sun exposure it allowed.

Sunscreen and skin care were far too important in Betty's daily regime to replace with a dark tan. Her roommate Kim, had visited the tanning salons prior to coming to Florida, and continued to do so at breaks during work hours. She always ensured lunch was on a patio or went to the beach and laid in a poor excuse for a bikini when Cameron was unavailable. Sun bathing was not a practice that Betty was even remotely interested in considering.

Her mum's brother had a bout with skin cancer that was a very tough road to fight, and was eventually lost after a very long, 15 years battle. Betty was 8 years old, when Uncle Sam was diagnosed, and her mum initially went overboard with skin protection for everyone. By the time Betty was in university, she was already beginning to see the signs of overexposure to the sun on her own age group when skin care was not a priority. Betty was always happy to report to her mum that sunscreen was a daily ritual, and often applied more than once, if out of the office.

Albany was lovely in the summer but the weather year-round did not always allow a walk in the sunshine. Plus, the distance, at the condo shared with Peter and then at her parents would have extended her commute to the office, to be more than an hour each way. Here in Florida, the rental unit and office are within 5 blocks and near enough to the waterfront that only a public transit bus ride of 10 minutes was required. Betty could never justify the expense of a car for herself. When Julia came, it was simple to either rent a car or just use a taxi. It had been Peter's car in Albany, although he never objected to her taking it for errands and when he left, she had relied on transit and Julia, while still in their condo. Living at her parents' home, she had used her mum's as needed and continued to use transit for work.

She would likely need to think of getting her own car as well as a home when leaving Florida. Perhaps something small but still good for the winter like the crossover model Julia had purchased a few years ago. Julia liked the bit of height difference when driving and the lift of the back provided great space on shopping trips. She would have to talk to her dad next week and get his input on new versus used. She could do her own research on the best type and then have great fun with Julia on test drives. She of course would return with her dad to close the deal and get the best price, as no one could negotiate a sale like her dad.

Betty settled into the planning of a spreadsheet for possible car options and drifts off herself. She was awakened by a scratching sound and looked around to orient herself with the strange surroundings. She then remembered the fear from this man laying next her and barely shifted to find the source of the noise. It was hard to not jump when she saw a thin black snake coming from under the door, but then as she became more aware, she realised it was not a snake but a fibre optic camera device. Someone outside was checking on them! Her movement caused David to pull her closer to him. She squeezed back very hard, hoping he would recognise her message to stay quiet.

But he did not stay still or quiet. Instead, he rolled over on top of her and proceeded with a kiss that left Betty thankful not to be standing. His touch was so soft yet drawing. Her knees would have buckled for sure. He broke off the kiss and moved to her neck with his face away from the room entrance. Betty began to squirm with both fright and stirrings of physical excitement. Should he touch a sensitive spot or breathe into her ear she would be like a lump of clay, at his will.

Thankfully instead, he whispered, "It's a camera, they don't think I am aware, but they do this almost every morning to see if I am still sleeping and to ensure the room is clear. Just be thankful they have not come in to make sure I am ok. Seeing us still in bed like this will cause them to back off very quickly. Just watch for the camera to leave if you can."

Betty was able to muster a bit of a squeak to indicate her understanding and managed to shift her vision, by kissing his rather large and delicious shoulder, to get a better view of the door. Sure, enough the camera snake was retreating from the room. As she watched to ensure that it was completely gone she noticed that his weight was becoming more pronounced. Almost to the point of suffocation.

But when she told him it was gone, he immediately flopped back into his old space and with his eyes closed, "I do apologise for the kiss and my behaviour, but needed them to leave."

Betty gathered her own thoughts enough to respond that she understood, but when he did not respond in return, she sat up to look closely at him only to find that, he was again asleep.

Betty touched his forehead to check for a fever and was relieved to note the beautiful golden skin was the same warmth as his shoulder. She got up and gathered her underwear on the way to the bathroom. She kept her movements soft and closed the bathroom door very quietly not wanting to disturb David's sleep and mostly not wanting to call the attention of whoever was on the other side of the bedroom door.

Why would anyone want to harm the owner of a pipeline company? And why did he have, what were clearly guards? And most importantly, why were these guards not watching him closer last night?

Betty found everything in the bathroom, that she needed for a female guest and wondered how often or how many there were. He was far too handsome and appeared to be a gentleman so he likely did not have any issues getting a date. The products being generic, obviously clarified there was no specific girlfriend or partner. Nice to know that there will not be a scrappy or possessive girlfriend to add to this bizarre situation.

When Betty returned from the bathroom and David was awake again. "How are you feeling? Your fever seems to be gone when I touched you. Do you have a headache? Need more water?" Betty knew she was rambling. The more David woke, the more he tried to sit up in bed, causing the sheet covering him to slide off more. Betty had seen male portraits and sculptures, had even lived intimately with a man, but she had never seen anything this perfectly beautiful. It was like

Da Vinci had carefully moulded a perfected *David* just for her viewing.

David had no clue what he looked like. His mind was still a bit foggy and he was thirsty, but the stomach rolls had subsided. He was just thankful not to be alone. "You stayed with me all night! I will never be able to thank you." His tone was genuine. "I would like more water if there is any left."

Betty had to swallow hard to take in more air. This was actual kindness and true thankfulness. "Of course, there is more let me grab you one." She happily popped back in to the bathroom to retrieve a fresh bottle.

Handing it to David, he attempted the twist of the plastic lid and quickly handed it back to Betty. "I guess it will take a bit to recover my strength. If you could please help me?"

Betty easily removed the cap and handed back the full bottle. "Are you ok sitting up?"

David took a greedy drink and then seeing, she was just about to remind him to sip as she had last night, tipped the bottle in a toast and proceeded to consume over half of the bottle with delicate sips. "I needed that, but now need to visit that room myself." Pointing to the bathroom.

He was already removing the sheet, preparing to stand when Betty breathed a sigh of relief seeing the boxer shorts covering him. "Do you need help up?" Hoping she would not have to get much closer to that barely covered form.

David swung his feet to the floor and sat for a moment on the edge of the bed. He then rose to a standing position and reached out to for the wall adding additional support. "I appreciate your help but would again like to try this myself. I promise not to faint and crack my head open. You can relax."

Continuing to use the wall as support David carefully moved into the bathroom, closing the door behind.

Betty sat on the edge of the bed and almost shot up like a firecracker when the door re-opened. David was a little pale again from the excursion, but instead of weariness he had a smile like a toddler using the toilet for the first time on his own. "You can relax Mum, I did just fine and even flushed, the toilet and thoroughly washed my hands."

His ability to joke calmed Betty down instantly. "I think you should lie down again. I will run down to the kitchen and see what I can get for food. Something soft and easy on your stomach is necessary, but you need food to get your strength back." Betty turned back towards the bathroom, intending to follow the path of the back stairs to the kitchen.

"Wait! No need to go anywhere. In fact, best if you don't." He reached for the phone on his bedside table. "What do you like for breakfast? They will send it up."

Oh, just have it sent up. No big deal. Just like ordering room service in a fancy hotel. "Excuse me? You have a cook? Plus, staff that will make whatever I want and then deliver it to your bedroom!" Betty's voice was rising without her even being aware.

"Calm down." David was trying to hush her back to a regular level of speaking. "I do not need the guards coming through that door. And yes, I have cook, and a maid. They are wives of the guards. The grounds keeper is the husband of my one female guard. Easier to employ a couple plus reduces leaks to the press."

"This is very new to me. Sorry, I have only had room service in a hotel. Even paying for the service I felt selfish and indulgent." Betty was used to herself preparing meals or her

71

mum prepared them. Eating out had always been a treat and room service an even greater treat.

"You are anything but selfish, that is clear from taking care of me last night. However, it is my life and household so best to not give them any cause to question why you are in my bedroom. Coffee, eggs, toast, bacon?" David had such logic with wealth, but appreciated and respected her reluctance to take advantage.

Betty shook her head to clear voices telling her he was wrong. "Yogurt, fruit and coffee if possible, would be lovely."

David saw her struggle and also saw, that was not an act, causing him to admire her even more, if that was even possible. "Can I have eggs if they are soft?"

"Yes." Feeling like a hardnosed nurse she could not stop adding. "Just no bacon or sausage as I think they may be too much for your stomach to manage. Cranberry juice and ginger or mint tea to drink will help with the washing out the poison and keep your kidneys happier than coffee."

"I love coffee! But you are right and I am in no position to ignore your opinion." David punched a button on the phone and then very politely placed the order, asking it to be served on his balcony when ready.

Betty started to tidy the room and then began to panic with only wearing his t-shirt. David smiled at her and walked to the closet retrieving a dark robe for himself and a white one for her. "Here, put this on. Leave the room as it is as I want the maid to be able to confirm our tryst, as such. I saw that you put the medical supplies away, thanks for that. There is an outside access to the balcony they will use to serve breakfast and I will have the room picked up, but not the bed linen changed, as that would be obvious, while we have breakfast."

Betty took the robe and wrapped herself in the soft satin material. Such luxury to feel on my skin. I need to add this to my list of items for a new home. It was touching the floor and the sleeves had to be rolled up, but still perfect to wear. "Thanks." Was her simple response while still touching the wonderful fabric.

David was still amazed that she was so easy to please. It was sad to see her slender, yet toned legs covered. "Can I suggest the removal of the t-shirt? It will add to the costume, as I am sorry to tell you that we will be on full display sitting on that balcony with a zoom lens."

"Are you kidding me?" Betty's eyes went wide at the idea of being under such scrutiny.

"Please just humour me." David was trying to be calming. "Once breakfast is finished and the room is cleaned, we can come back in and talk more. I feel that I owe you much more of an explanation and am sorry to say may need your assistance all weekend to sort this out."

"All weekend! No, I need to go home. I have errands and laundry, and… stuff." This was ridiculous!

"I am sorry, but once I explain things after breakfast it may help you understand. Will your roommate call the police?" David was suddenly concerned there could be a search for her.

"I doubt she will even miss me or notice I have been absent. We came here together last night, but other than occasionally walking to work, we do nothing together. She runs in a very different circle than I." Betty rarely saw Kim on weekends, so her statement to David was true.

"Well, that is good, one less thing to worry about. Look, I am very sorry, but I have to insist that you stay! No that is wrong, I have no right to insist anything from you. I am begging you to stay and help me sort this out. Please!" David was next, going to go for the offer of payment for her time, but her look confirmed his honesty had been the best approach.

With a very audible sigh Betty looked into his wonderful brown eyes, to see the truth that, he was truly concerned. "Ok, stop with the puppy look. It is unbecoming on someone of your position." And with that they both smiled. "But I am not interested in wearing just this robe all weekend and putting my dress on from last night is hardly appropriate."

"I think I can work with that as well." Looking on the balcony and noticing the activity of food being set up David motioned Betty towards the patio doors. "Let's enjoy our breakfast first and then we can come back into privacy and work out clues, clothing and other details."

Chapter 6

Acknowledging the rumblings in her own tummy, she moved with him to the balcony. David opened the doors and escorted her out of the room and seated her like a couple on their honeymoon. The soft nuzzle to her ear caused a blush from her toes to the top of her head. How could she possibly keep things logical when he continued to throw these curve balls?

He seated himself after returning to the room to unlock the door and providing the maid with clear instructions, Betty was redder, if possible, at the realisation that this was all for show. It would be so nice to have a partner that came to the breakfast table every morning with such a show of affection. Her own father had always had a kiss and comment of love for her mum, not just in the morning, but throughout the day for nothing particular. It was moving back home and seeing this display of genuine affection first hand, had helped Betty realise that Peter had never shown her this form of appreciation in their relationship.

The coffee and teapot were set in front of two brilliantly yellow mugs. Until looking at the mugs, Betty was unaware of the care put in to set up the tray with cheery yellow stoneware and a matching yellow rose set in a clear heavy glass vase. The napkins were a pale-yellow damask cloth that had been ironed and folded with such care, she felt almost guilty breaking one, for David and then herself. The setting of the pots allowed Betty to pour the hot beverages and serve food with the appearance of taking the tea and leaving David his coffee to enjoy.

Enjoying the light breakfast and the amazing coffee Betty relaxed into the warmth of the morning sun. David was eating with reserve even though, she could see that he really just wanted to inhale the offering. Remembering that they were likely under a telescope Betty viewed the grounds and tried to keep the conversation light. "I walked around a bit last evening before meeting you and knew that you had direct access to the water. I did not realise the extent of your lot, or the beauty and care of the grounds."

David was thankful for her quick ability to find a topic of general discussion, easily slipped into a discussion of his appreciation for the grounds keeper's care. Even being so bold as to suggest a stroll on the grounds after some additional time alone. This only caused another blush for Betty. Having people think she was here for sex was demeaning regardless of maintaining the necessity of the ruse.

He apologised for not knowing the names of all the flowers and trees. Betty looked over and understood that his thoughts were still not clear as a result of the drug and offered a comment of not really being that interested in gardening, rather she just preferred to enjoy others' work. Good grief Betty thought to herself, could she be providing any worse of an opinion of herself to the staff?

With most of his plate cleared, David leaned over in a show of again nuzzling her neck. "Between the heat out here and my level of weakness I really need to lie down again. Can you please continue the show and put your arms around me to help me stand? That way if I stumble it will just look like awkward sexual tension."

The blush returned as a vibrant red against the brilliant white of her robe. David smiled at her heated skin with a sigh when he lifted his head from her neck. Betty wondered if this could possibly get any more humiliating, but figured she was currently in for a penny, may as well be in for a pound.

"I think we should spare the staff and take this back inside." And reaching for David's waist they both began to rise from their chairs.

David did lean forward too much and covered it by pressing a kiss to her forehead. Wishing it was real affection Betty reached around his waist and linked her hand into his opposite hand to continue moving towards the patio entrance returning to their cocoon.

Once back inside, the bedroom David released his hold on Betty and slowly made his way back to the bed. "Please make sure the doors are locked and draw the curtains on that patio door. The window over the bed does not have a direct view but the patio does." And with all his remaining effort, flopped on the bed with a sign of relief.

Betty wandered in the room as tasked, and brought a new bottle of water from under the bathroom counter. "I would still like to see you drink more water today if you can. I am hoping that it will continue to wash out any residual effects of the drug. I am almost out of battery on my phone so don't want to use it to check the internet again."

David took the water and patted the edge of the bed as an indication for Betty to sit. "I sincerely appreciate your assistance and acting. I promise to make this up to you and will ensure you are properly rewarded."

"Like money! I don't need to be paid to help you." Betty was insulted at the money offer, having people view her character as anything less than beyond reproach was huge. "But, having the story come out truthfully with your staff would be nice. At least, they won't look at me like a hooker when I leave."

"Ok, relax, no more offers to pay, but I will be replacing that dress and hopefully with one that looks as lovely on you as that did last night." David looked over at the limp and crumpled silk dress and jacket hung up by the maid.

Betty looked over at it as well. "I loved that dress when I bought it and was very happy wearing it last night but to be honest, did not even want to attend. I did have plans of many more occasions to wear it. I will have it professionally cleaned and pressed and maybe it will be lovely again."

David reached for her hand, causing the lovely doe eyes to look at him as they had all last evening. "It was not just the dress that was lovely, it was you as well and I am most grateful that you were here and have not bolted on me so far. I will make all of this up to you somehow, and that is a true promise."

Betty was rather shocked by his comment. All she could do was nod in agreement to his statement, forcing her eyes not to mist over with emotion. The situation they were in was enough of a strain, but constantly being set off guard by his actions was beginning to cause the thread she had been hanging onto, to show signs of unravelling. Not a big surprise as she acknowledged the lack of sleep, on top of the fear

David may have truly been in need of professional medical assistance.

David was still holding her hand. "You look as tired as I feel. Do you want to lie down and close your eyes for a few minutes before we try to sort out this mess, I have placed us in?"

"No, you get comfortable." The thought of lying in bed again with this physical specimen as more than her nerves could manage. "Is there a pen and paper in here? I can write out what we know from your memory last night and then after your nap we can try to fill in gaps from there."

David reached for another pillow to bunch under his head. Betty reacted as dutiful nurse and finished the reach causing her robe to shift exposing the lovely skin that provided warmth last night. He dared to hope that when this threat was over, he would be allowed to properly charm her into willingly exposing that skin to his vision and touch. David sighed at the thought and was for once thankful that his body was too weak to respond as a healthy male. "There should be both in the drawer of that table beside the sofa."

Betty rose to find the items, but rather than returning to perch on the side of the bed, instead sprawled out on the sofa with her feet up, still turned to view David from a safe distance. She began writing, in point form, their discussion last evening when she identified the drug, read out each point and asked if David had more to add. But by the fifth point he was drifting off to sleep again, so Betty continued not expecting any answers from across the room.

Her conclusion was, the need to identify the young couple that shared the pineapple and if they were working alone or with assistance from others or his staff. Running these possible scenarios through her mind Betty drifted off to be again awakened abruptly, this time from the phone beside the bed.

David answered with a gruff response, and proceeded to only provide short answers of "No... I am sure... Dinner served on the patio again would be lovely... 5:00 p.m. would be great... Thank you." Hanging up the phone, David looked at the clock on his bedside table and was a little shocked to see that it was already 3:30 p.m. "Sorry that woke you up." He looked over at Betty thinking that, across the room was much too far away. "Apparently, we both needed a nap. Dinner will be served at 5:00 p.m. on the patio."

"I gathered that from the call. I don't suppose it would be possible for me to run home and get some other clothes?" Betty was rather hoping to dispense with the robe and have not only fresh underwear, but her own coverings to show she was not just a sex object for this man.

"I would really prefer that you not leave until we have a better handle on what happened. I know that is very selfish of me, but let's talk until dinner and hope we can have some better answers. I don't know your size, but thinking the ladies on the property would have some things that would not be too uncomfortable. I do however, like you in my robe and t-shirt, so would be happy to lend you another if that would help." David added a grin to his sly reply.

The sheepish look on his face was his only salvation. Betty was thinking this was rather forward until she saw he was just teasing her. She actually smiled in return and then continued in true business form. "Ok, I wrote down what I remember from last night after you nodded off. I also noted a few questions that may probe your memory and give us answers." Betty swung her feet to the floor and stood with a stretch. "I will get us more water and then we need to tackle this with as much detail as possible."

With Betty retiring to the bathroom, David slowly got up from the bed. Between breakfast and the nap, his headache and fuzzy mind had cleared. But standing upright, the light-headed feeling returned after a few moments as a reminder he was not clear of the drug from last night.

Betty returned with new water bottles and David took his turn in the bathroom. When he came back into the bedroom, Betty was seated in the large tub chair, across from the sofa with pen and a notepad poised for action. "I thought you might prefer to stretch out on the sofa."

"Appreciate that." David lay down again, as suggested and reached for his water bottle to continue the liquid purge.

Betty reviewed her notes and then started in with the points and a check marked to indicate as correct. She then moved on to the questions. His description of the couple that provided the pineapple left her cold and slightly nauseous. David watched as the pen slid from her hand and the note pad drops to the floor. "What is it? Are you sick? Did I somehow poison you?" David was up from the sofa and knelt at her feet by the time his words finished tumbling from his mouth.

Betty looked at his worried face, both amazed and surprised he had moved so quickly. There was a surreal feeling, seeing him there. His look was one of concern and she could see he was talking but, for some unknown reason, she had no ability to hear. Instead, what continued looping through her mind was the look of her roommate and date as they had walked to Cameron's car the night before. Betty felt the pressure of his hand squeezing her own and finally came back to the present of David's bedroom. She shook off his hand. "Sorry, I spaced out there for a bit. But, are you sure on the description of the couple?"

"Well, the light was a bit dim, so the colour of the clothing could be off, but the build of both and blonde hair was accurate." David was thinking she still looked a bit pale, but her eyes were back into focus and her cheeks were turning pink again.

"Give me the paper and pen, I need to ensure we have it written down as accurately as possible. And get up off your knees, you look silly." Trying to recover from being shaken by his description she continued. "Accuracy is the detail needed, because you just described my roommate and her boyfriend."

As Betty noted in detail the description provided by David, they discussed how she came to the party, with Kim and the boyfriend, Cameron. She could provide more information on Kim and was sure that a call to Bart Hartley in Albany, could fill in any other details from personnel files. The unknown remained on who Cameron was. Betty could not even recall a last name, only that they had been dating for a few months.

David's thoughts moved to logical thinking as well and he asked Betty if there was a possibility that the other people in his office at MDP had been acting strange or questioning more than their position would require. Betty was still feeling a little shocked with Kim's involvement, but could not recall anything more to add.

David took a deep breath and looked directly at Betty. "You have proven your trust by caring for me last evening and continuing the ruse today. All that you shared last night leads me to believe, that I can share similar information with you and trust not to find it in the press after you leave here."

Betty only nodded in response. David took a long drink of water and cleared his throat before continuing. "My real name is Celestino Davide Baffa, and living here in the USA, I have shortened it to David Baffa. My family is from Calabria in Southern Italy. Our family has a huge corporation in Europe and my ownership of MDP is the first of our branching into North America and then adding real estate. My success with MDP and with the implementation of the new software system will allow for added acquisitions and expansion."

"It is the expansion that is not being taken well by some rival companies and in the last year I have received a few threats on my life." The look of shock on Betty's face caused David to raise his hand to stop her interruption and continue. "You can relax as none were credible, so my team of guards stepped up their awareness. The staff at the house was expanded to include the couples, as I said earlier. Now I am sure someone is after me, as seen last night, the threats have been stepped up to action. If it is ok with you, I am going to call in my three-security team to fill them in." As Betty was still only nodding with stunned amazement, David moved to the phone and began a call.

Betty heard him talking to someone on the other end of the call and was rather shocked when he asked for full casual clothing for his lady guest, including *intimates*. He looked at Betty and said, a size six with a look of question at Betty. She only nodded in stunned recognition, that he so accurately guessed her size. Thankfully, he did not ask for her correct bra size as, that would have likely put her into a full state of embarrassment again. That seemed to be happening on a regular basis in the short time with this man.

His strength was clearly returning as the skin tone was back to a healthy bronze colour. His deep brown eyes now showed a sparkle of light, as opposed to the pools of despair when begging for help last evening. Last night his mouth had often been pressed closed and his jaw clamped in containment, of the nausea and cramping caused by the drug, was now relaxed to sit as a finely polished jaw line. The Roman nose that had stood out last night in the throes of illness, seemed to recede with relaxation of the facial muscles, and his previous taunt mouth had returned to reveal rather full lips that were quick to turn upwards at the corners, in generous smiles.

Following his call David retired to the bathroom and Betty was left to review her notes. If the security team was going to be involved now, she would ensure that everything was properly prepared to be handed over, before she left to go home at the conclusion of the meeting. She had nothing more of value to add and was happy to leave this to professionals.

Betty was still reviewing her notes when the knock sounded on the door. Before she could rise to answer, David emerged from the bathroom fully dressed and moved to the door, she did not recall him taking a change of clothing into the bathroom. He gestured for her to remain seated and leaned over to remove the towel left at the door jam. She saw him briefly lean against the door, proving he was not entirely well, stronger for sure, but not fully recovered.

Opening the door, he invited the 3-waiting staff into the bedroom. They each entered like children finally allowed into a candy store. Their eyes were roaming the room to take in every detail. Knowing the room was secure they looked David over completely and then as if the timing were practiced daily, all three settled their gaze on Betty, causing yet another flush of red to rise from her toes to the top of her head.

David continued to be fascinated with the flush of embarrassment Betty constantly displayed. But rather than subject her to the continued scrutiny by his team he stepped beside her, as a sign of defence and began the introductions. "This tall mass of muscles is Josh." Josh nodded with a weak smile, still very guarded to the situation. "Josh is ex-military and is married to our wonderful cook Sally. She quickly found that her nerves were not suited to fast paced restaurant work, so was more than happy to take over my kitchen."

"Next, we have Naldo, also former military, as it was his quickest way to gain citizenship for himself and his wife Pirro, who manages the household organisation and cleaning." Naldo, with his dark Cuban looks, released much of Betty's tension with a brilliant wide smile of welcome. "Finally, we come to Jennifer, ex-police and married to our wonderful grounds keeper, Arlo." Jennifer was small compared to the other team members, but her eyes were continuing to assess any threat while she smiled at Betty.

Jennifer stepped towards Betty, offering a stack of folded garments. "I grabbed a full set of yoga clothing, hoping that even if the size was not correct it would still be comfortable."

Taking the offered stack after standing up from her chair, Betty smiled at the realisation that they were likely similar in size. "Thank you, I really appreciate having some clothing to wear other than my rumpled dress from last night." Betty gestured to the now sad dress that was hung earlier by Pirro.

David wanted to get on with the meeting and without intending to be exclusionary asked Betty to leave. "Betty, why don't you take those items and treat yourself to a lovely bath while I talk to my team."

Betty was a little taken back that this was not a question of her wanting a bath, but a clear statement of dismissal. Stuttering slightly, she hands her note pad to Jennifer in return for the clothing. "Um… These are my notes so hope they help." And without a look at David, dashed for the bathroom. With the door locked to the bedroom, she leans against the wall, first in embarrassment for her appearance and then in anger for being dismissed. "Well fine!" She muttered to herself and laid out items to enjoy a refreshing shower.

Stepping from the shower, she felt very clean and refreshed, Betty looked longingly at the beautiful bathtub set in marble. "I may not get to enjoy you." Addressing the tub like a person. "But when this is over, I intend to treat myself to a staycation at a fancy hotel and spend hours soaking away all memories of these past two days." Betty dried her hair and was pleased to find the clothing was wonderfully comfortable. She never went to yoga classes at home nor bought any of the outfits made popular by *Lululemon*.

She and Julia would have to make this a priority, when she got home, plus a great shopping plan on Julia's next visit. Jennifer had included a sports bra that was surprisingly supportive while being comfortable, a brilliant solution to needing a bra size. There were even soft-soled shoes that would allow Betty to go home in this outfit without having to put on her beige heels that were far better suited to a dress.

Chapter 7

Feeling fully refreshed and clothed, Betty returned to the bedroom, to find only Jennifer and David remaining. Both looked up as she entered the room and rather than being dismissed as she had earlier, Jennifer patted the cushion on the opposite end of the sofa, where she sat. "Looks like everything fit. Please join us, as I would like to once more review your notes. Which, are the best detail I have ever encountered, by the way!"

Betty smiled at the compliment, but rather than moving to the sofa turned her gaze towards David. He immediately understood the look, and after having been taken to task by Jennifer, on Betty's earlier dismissal to the bathroom David knew he owed Betty more than just an apology. Meeting her gaze, "I am so sorry after all that you have done to have not included you with an update to my security team."

"I was just trying to let you get changed as I know you have been uncomfortable in my robe. I have explained everything to the team, and they will also explain to the others that you have been caring for me. Jennifer still has questions if you are willing to help." David looked imploringly at Betty and then to Jennifer. "Did I miss anything?"

Jennifer laughed and again patted the cushion. "That was a start, David. We all owe this lady a lot, for taking care of you and not bolting from the house screaming last night, or this morning." Jennifer touched Betty's hand as a gesture of appreciation when Betty finally settled on the sofa.

"Thanks for the clothing, it is really lovely and I need to get my own outfit. I had no idea what I have been missing out on. I may even take up yoga." Betty only addressed Jennifer and this slight was not missed by David.

Jennifer caught it as well and re-covered quickly by sticking to the business of the situation. "So, Josh and Naldo have gone to continue investigations on the street and see who this boyfriend of your roommate really is. Your notes are again wonderfully detailed. I have a computer program that can do facial drawings if you are willing to help us identify him. Also, wanted to say that was brilliant research in figuring out the poison source was Jimsonweed. Doing my own research, I have to agree and also agree with how you forced the water."

Betty only responded with a weak. 'Yes' to both helping and acknowledgment of her diagnosis.

David stepped back into the conversation from his position in the tub chair, across from the sofa. "I too am very thankful you are so focused on detail. I have talked to the team and while the other threats to date were not credible, there was no threat this time, which makes the team nervous. There is an acquisition meeting scheduled for this coming Monday, and clearly the goal was for me to be unable to attend thereby forfeiting my bid for ownership. I also know that you really want to go home but would like to ask you to please stay until tomorrow and help Jennifer identify this, Cameron."

Betty was torn. David is not being demanding. No sly, puppy dog eyes. He was not telling her she had to stay at this house another night. He was asking. And not just asking, but telling her why he was asking. As much as Betty waned to be back in her condo and leave this unbelievable event behind, she looked up at David's dark eyes. "Yes, I will stay and help."

She was about to ask more questions, when the sounds on the patio indicated dinner being served. Jennifer rose from the sofa and pulled the curtains aside to confirm. "Your dinner is here. I am going to catch up with Josh and Naldo plus begin my own searches. Enjoy your dinner and let me know when you want to start with a composite picture."

David also rose and offered his hand to Betty, to join him for dinner. He thanked Jennifer and escorted Betty onto the patio, without a care of the bedroom door being closed. Betty sat down to a lovely place setting again with china and linens, this time with blue tones. Too early for candlelight, there was a small arrangement of fresh flowers, likely having been picked from Alro's well-tended flowerbeds. The roasted chicken, Spanish rice and grilled vegetables were amazing.

Being far hungrier than she thought she was, when first seated, she was rather shocked to discover that between David and herself, not a morsel of food remained. Sally had left a note, that coffee and dessert could be served later so as not to interfere with David's digestion, leaving the couple to enjoy the evening view of the water.

Betty was more relaxed with this second meal on the patio. The staff clearly no longer viewed her as some sex object holed up in David's room. She began to think that another evening here would be fine, after all it would be spent helping Jennifer and then heading home in the morning to prepare for work on Monday. However, the calm was not to be. David reached for her hand and drew it to his lips in a romantic gesture. He then leaned forward pulling her into him.

Betty looked up into his eyes, with his returning health, showing brilliant crystal sheen to them in the lowering sun. She swallowed deeply to remind her system to breathe. No acting for the staff with this gesture. Was this amazing man actually looking at her with love and desire?

Nope! The bubble of joy filling Betty's head burst like sticky gum on a child's face. David still smiled but his words were not at all matching his romantic gestures. "There is a sail boat in the water that has a long-range lens pointed at us. I am sorry to ask for your continued acting skills. We can watch a romantic sunset on the water, or move back inside, your choice?"

Betty felt the over feeding of Sally's cooking turn to stone in her tummy. How could she be such a fool to think, that a man as handsome and wealthy as David Baffa would want plain old Betty McDowell from upstate New York? "Let's enjoy the sunset for a bit." She did truly enjoy the sunsets in Miami, as the fire and heat of the day melted into the water with a final surge of reds and orange. Knowing her time in Florida was limited, and the view from her condo was not nearly as impressive as David's patio on the waterfront. She could enjoy both the view and the feel of being held in those wonderfully sculpted arms, even if it was only acting.

Dreaming was part of acting to achieve melding into your assumed character. Immersing yourself into your character had been drilled into all of the class by the talented school drama teacher. Mr Bains had been brushed over by Broadway and off Broadway as a talented director, but the Discovery Academy filled his ego with both praise and tenure each term. Betty and Julia had giggled and laughed through his classes but the lessons were drilled home as was every class Betty attended. She would play her role to perfection, not for David, but in memory of Mr Bains.

Chapter 8

Jennifer da Silva, sat behind the computer screen on her assigned desk. The security team had developed the basement of the lovely estate home, into a high-tech operation that would rival most professional firms. Each office was open onto the team war room with a smart conference table and a huge wall screen to display items needing sharing. Behind each office was a private sitting room then bed/bath for the couple. The common space of the house was open to the couples anytime, but it was thoughtful of David to allow the private space as well. Jennifer and Arlo preferred the warmth of the kitchen and patio with the other couples. Arlo loved his work of caring for the property, but in the evenings, also valued the time to relax and enjoy his efforts with the new family he had made.

Both Josh and Naldo were ex-military and both had intelligence backgrounds so the move to private security was rather natural following their release from the United States Military service. Their expertise and contacts continued to be of value in their protection of the Baffa Corporation and David's person. The programs and supporting network used by the security team allowed for extensive information searches as did the continual reporting of search algorithms developed by Naldo, her team member.

Jennifer as a young detective with the Miami Dade Police had felt very fortunate to be partnered with a 20 year, highly decorated, and greatly admired detective. Jimmy Gates, was in his mid-40s when Jennifer was moved to the organised crime task force. Jimmy was ending his second marriage so had nothing but time and energy to pour into a beautiful young detective, willing to be moulded.

Jimmy picked her up each morning, they shared every meal and followed each lead on the street or in the office until he dropped her off in the evening. It had been Jimmy, that taught Jennifer how to search the internet and databases for valued information, introduced her to contacts within and outside of the department for additional sources. Jimmy had many street sources as well, and they were shared and developed as a team with Jennifer being mentored like a prodigy.

Their bond grew and developed naturally so it was not even a surprise following the successful bust of a high valued drug ring that Jimmy walked into her apartment that night instead of simply dropping her off. By the end of that week, Jimmy had moved into her apartment with boxes from his now second ex-wife's home that never seemed to get unpacked. But Jennifer felt like the luckiest girl in the world. She was in love with a man that shared everything with her both day and night.

There were always rumours in the office. Jennifer had learned in the squad room to ignore most of them unless they were tied to a case. Her floating on a cloud made her oblivious to the whispers and rude gestures behind her back by other team members. One older lady, Gwen, in the office tried to talk to Jennifer in the coffee room after the second week, but Jennifer could not and would not hear the noise of an old bag that was likely jealous of Jennifer's youth and clear path for advancement with Jimmy by her side.

As Jennifer now watched the spinning icon on her computer screen, she reflected on Gwen's rebuff of what was clearly only intended as a warning. Jennifer was too young and sure of her position to heed the warnings of an older female. But it had been Gwen, that had sat on the floor of the ladies washroom and held Jennifer while she sobbed after an intense berating by the Assistant District Attorney following a failed arrest.

Not only had the suspects gotten away, but it was becoming evident that there had been a tip off to the illicit crew. Jimmy had skated through his own private interrogation and had dumped all blame and responsibility on Jennifer. Jennifer had been given what she thought was the lead at the time, but instead had been clearly set up by the other members of the task force that were fed up with the *Double J* team as they were called in private.

But Jimmy had been far more astute to the rumour mill and in seeing the writing on the wall that his career would only be hindered by the beautiful and delicious Jennifer, had set events in motion that would allow for his clean exit. He had heard of a promotion to Tampa and with the cost of two alimony payments, could not afford to miss the opportunity of an offer. Jimmy knew from one of his sources, that the crew would move their operation to the other coast following the failed bust, so had laid out this information to enhance his own move, while leaving Jennifer to mop up the mess.

Before the day was over, Jimmy was on a plane to Tampa and Jennifer was stripped of her gun and shield and escorted from the building with the threat of pending charges, should they find she was the leak. She had arrived back at her apartment, and in fumbling to pay the driver when exiting the cab had caused the box of her few desk items to spill onto the sidewalk. The cabby sensed desperation and had no intention of becoming part of that hot mess so pleaded urgency to another fare. Jennifer gathered up the contents and stood only to slam into the solid body of the gardener for the complex.

Instead of apologising and moving inside, Jennifer had snapped, the last thread holding her together and in loud sobs began sinking onto the sidewalk. The strong arms that held her upright included, a soothing voice that asked which her unit was. Guiding her to the door and then asking for her keys, causing Jennifer to finally look into the dark handsome face that was peering at her. She pulled the keys from her pocket, as she never took a purse to work and offered them to a hand that was rough from labour, but delivered a gentle touch.

Finally, inside and seated on the sofa, Jennifer looked up when a glass of water was pushed at her hands. "Who are you?"

"I am Arlo, the gardener for this complex." A simple explanation and followed with a genuine smile that Jennifer had no choice but to weakly return.

Arlo spend the evening with her, he asked if there was someone to call and be with her. It was then that Jennifer had realised all of Jimmy's boxes were gone. Between sobbing and trying to drink the water, Arlo continued to force into her hands, she spilled out the past 6 months of her partnership ending with the events of the day.

He did not judge and only added in his confirmation of seeing her with Jimmy and knew she was a cop from the other residents in the complex. He told Jennifer that she was likely in shock from the day's events and told her to sleep if possible. He would be back in the morning for work and would check on her, if that was all right. It was fine with Jennifer, there was no one that really stood out to follow up on her care. Her self-involved parents were remarried to other self-involved individuals, and rarely even remembered she existed.

She had joined the police academy after high school in a state of rebellion to get her parent's attention. To her surprise, she loved the hard work and training and following graduation, loved police work. After yesterday, her brief career was over and it would be her parents with the last laugh, when she called for money. Jennifer had always lived simply after the lavish lifestyle with her parents, so her savings account was reasonable.

It was only thinking of her finances the next day that she realised Jimmy had not paid a cent when living with her. They had taken turns with takeout meals, just as they had before they lived together. Seeing his boxes gone, brought on a fresh batch of tears with the realisation, he had set her up and now she was alone.

Arlo did follow up on her wellbeing the next day and every day following, whether he was working on the property or not. For the first few weeks, his visits were brief and he only checked in. After the second week, he handed her the business card of a businessman that was a client of his family's landscaping firm. "He is looking to add a female to his security team."

It took Jennifer another day to place the call. She had expected a voice mail rather than the real person and after introducing herself, the voice on the other end said he had been waiting for her call. She not only met with the businessman, David Baffa, but had a job offer the day following the meeting. She was planning to ask Arlo out as a thank you for the job lead, but he beat her to it by asking her to dinner to celebrate the news.

Jennifer had asked Mr Baffa to delay her start date giving the time to release her apartment, as she would be moving to the Baffa home with the other members of the security team. She had also planned a visit with each parent, but was once again disappointed to find them both unavailable.

Arlo continued to see Jennifer every day, sometimes a formal date and sometimes just a quick visit. The day she moved into the Baffa home, was also the first time she slept with Arlo. It had been a fun day moving. She had donated or sold most of her furniture and household items, as her new room contained much better furnishings. Arlo was bringing in the last load, when she moved out from behind the door, not realising he was there.

The boxes he was carrying fell when the door rapped his shoulder. She had made the mistake of laughing as he rubbed the bruised spot and then sobered up with his casual remark. "It is a good thing I love you, or you would be on the floor with those boxes."

Jennifer was stunned at first. They had grown closer over the past month and feelings were changing rapidly for her. His kisses had been both dreamy and dazzling, but her mind continued to pull her back, it being too soon after Jimmy. His statement of love, was the first she had ever heard. Her own parents had never said this to her, and Jimmy certainly never had. But this wonderful man who showed her only kindness, compassion, friendship and romance was now showing her love.

Their love only grew from that day forward. Jennifer had no idea what truly sharing in love meant, until Arlo. When they announced their simple courthouse wedding ceremony three months later, both sides of their families were not only shocked, but also rude and unforgiving. It was their new family, at the house, that was not surprised and instead of recriminations, held a private party of celebration for the new couple.

It was this family unit she was now focused on protecting. Being called to David's room this afternoon had significantly allowed her and the entire staff to calm down. She laughed at herself, as she remembered telling Josh, that if David did not let them into the room by dinnertime she would be kicking in the door. Her statement had been said over coffee in the kitchen with Sally and Arlo present. Arlo had strongly suggested she rethink that option as he really liked this home and family, and that approach may truly be a bell she could not un-ring.

Why was that man so logical, right and then topped it off by being loving? No fighting, no argument, just his simple, but logical, statement and then he wrapped his strong arms around her, to give her the calming strength she needed.

Sally on the other hand, had been in line with Jennifer. Sally stated that she would be standing right behind Jen, when the door was kicked in, but Josh had agreed with Arlo. So, to calm herself down, Sally spent the day cooking and baking. The guys were thrilled with the cookies and pies, Jennifer would need too much time in the basement gym to burn off those calories, but a bite of each from Arlo's plate was enough to satisfy the cravings, and confirm once again just how talented Sally was in the kitchen.

Naldo and Pirro had their own way of dealing with the lack of information. He had been reviewing the security footage from the party to match the woman up in David's bedroom to the dress Pirro had taken pictures of when tiding the room. Naldo was doing searches, had a picture of the lady that had matched the patio pictures when they had brunch but still no information on who she was, until David invited them to the room.

Everyone in the house was relieved to learn the identity of the lady was of a contract employee of MDP, not a threat to their boss, and most importantly not some bimbo that Jennifer would have loved to bounce out the front door in a crumpled dress. Instead, she was actually looking forward to Pirro's suggestion of inviting Betty to join their private yoga classes, thinking it would be valuable for everyone to refocus on form and basics through teaching a newbie.

However, the threat of the poisoning needed to be solved and eliminated and then, she would have a private conversation with David. If he had any doubts on her loyalty or abilities, she would tender her resignation regardless, of the perks of the job and family. She would not stay in a position where she was not trusted or adding value. Her lessons with Jimmy were still too much of a reminder that personal integrity could never falter.

Chapter 9

The evening sitting out on the patio was a treasured time for Betty. Regardless of the reality of the arms holding her close, or the warmth and strength from the chest she leaned against, it was still a memory to be filed away.

The timing of actually having dinner had been delayed due to the security team discussion. Betty was enjoying the lateness of the sunset in Miami, as the colours danced on the water and melted into the waves. Darkness came before 6:00 p.m. in Albany this time of year, so sitting in the fading light after 8:00 p.m. was truly a treat.

David and she both noted that the boat had not moved anchor. There was no noted fishing spot or specific attraction or party that was causing the boat to remain. Both of David's neighbours were in their 80s and had been long-time residents of the area. As well as, David knew from Arlo, caring for the neighbour grounds, that both were away visiting family in other states.

Naldo and Arlo had dressed up in Arlo's working clothes and boots during dinner to make a display of cleaning up the beach. They used the utility Kubota to assist with cleaning up driftwood, which allowed the hidden camera to get an unobstructed view of the boat and its markings. Josh was in his office, adjusting the view and focus of the camera remotely and running searches on the results with each image.

Sally and Pirro spoke pleasantly with Betty when clearing the table and offering coffee and dessert. Betty did not want David having coffee just yet, and with her not walking or physical activity felt best to decline the dessert. Betty suggested a pot of chamomile tea for David in his room once they made their dramatic move indoors and the ladies agreed this was better for him than coffee. Even grumbling of missing his caffeine, he also had to agree.

With the table being cleared, David and Betty made a display for the lens on the boat, to move inside for the evening. It showed David's strength and him having a wonderfully indulgent weekend with a lady. When outside, this time David had shown to those in the know, that his strength was returning, providing a wonderful air of relief to all the staff.

Once back in the room, Betty drew the curtains for the large patio doors and David instantly relaxed. She could see he was truly more tired than appearing on the patio, but the completion of another scripted act was in the can, as the producers would say.

Betty was slipping on the yoga shoes and gathering her small bag, when David rather sheepishly asked. "Would you like to stay another night with me?"

Betty showed him her amazing smile. "As tempting as that would be, you need the rest and I promised to assist Jennifer following dinner. Also, the puppy dog eyes are beginning to wear thin."

"Well rats, now you sound like my mother telling me to 'stop it' when I challenge her with my look. Honestly, I feel very comfortable with you near me and will truly miss you across the hallway. Also, again, I thank you for not bolting out the door screaming and the team will greatly appreciate your assistance." David was being sincere, even when he wanted to gather her in his arms and beg her to stay forever.

"I appreciate the complement, but am sure you will sleep much better without me. We can talk again in the morning and see what your team is able to uncover overnight." Betty was almost relieved to be leaving this room and the tight spaces from David filling the room.

"Do not leave in the morning without saying goodbye." David was so tired he was afraid he would oversleep and miss another moment with her. He needed to suggest another intimate breakfast to continue the ruse, regardless, if truly necessary.

"I would not think of leaving without saying goodbye, but I will say good evening and find my room and then Jennifer. Sleep well David." Betty moved into the hallway not waiting for his reply. If he called her back, she would race to his side like there was a fire licking at her heels. Instead, all she heard in reply was David wishing her a good sleep as well. It may have been some time without a date or boyfriend, but she was not going to throw herself at a man that did not even want her.

While Betty walked away, David went through his routine of preparing for bed. He had never been so tired in his entire life and was actually happy to see the pot of tea and dish of sugar cookies that Sally had left on his bedside table. He snuggled in with a large mug in his hand, Sally knew he hated teacups and was just reaching for a cookie when he caught a whiff of Betty's remaining scent from the night before. He was pleased to have the forethought of only requesting Pirro make up the bed rather than changing the sheets. Now at least without her in his bed tonight, he could inhale her scent.

As he sipped his tea and enjoyed the always-delicious treat of even plain cookies, David began to consider how lonely he would be without Betty. In under 24 hours, she had not only entered his life, but taken over every aspect of his thought and decision-making. He laughed out loud, suddenly remembering his own father's comment on the celebration of the 25 Wedding Anniversary with his mother as a description of meeting her, but continuing to share this after all the years of their marriage. He also remembered the next statement his father had made while staring in to the dark eyes of his wife. "I did not become whole until you filled my life, and I will remain full forever with our love."

At the time, David had thought his father only a romantic Italian, but after these hours with Betty he was seeing a much deeper understanding of the truth of being with not only a lover but a partner forever.

David finished his snack and tea and had every intention of reading some of his files from the office before turning off the light. However, the tea and lingering effects of the Jimsonweed had the file dropping from his hand in minutes. His mind drifted in and out of dreams of Betty in his house, Betty at the office, Betty with his parents, Betty organising their children. Scenarios that showed a clear theme of Betty happy and effortlessly turning on that amazing smile she seemed to have been holding in reserve lately. But more than smiles and happiness, David constantly saw Betty at his side.

Betty had deposited her purse and the crumpled dress in the guest room across the hall from David. Wandering to the lower level to find Jennifer, she stood at the top of the beautiful stairway that had been a missed opportunity the night before. There was no crowd or security in place, which she now knew as Naldo and Josh. Leaning at the curved upper balcony looking down on the expansive entryway it was more beautiful than noted last evening now absent of added bodies filling the space.

While the railing was finely crafted wrought iron, what had been missed on her original look was the single strip of inlaid white crystal. It was not as heavy as mother of pearl, and not as clear as glass. With closer inspection, she discovered it was intricately laid pieces of smoky quartz. The craftsmanship was so precise, that it was hard to discover the seams where pieces were joined.

Betty was reminded of the stained-glass dome above with the light and faint traces of colour flowing in with the light of the moon. Looking up, she saw the same iron used in the banister was also holding the colourful glass pieces in place. The dome window design was a simple gold star surrounded by turquoise fill for the first circle.

The second circle held rough shaped rose buds in vibrant red, leaves of green and filled with a light sky blue. The final surrounding circle boarder was a broken design of Arabesque blue-purple. Betty stared at the lovely, yet simple, design and wondered just how old the window truly was. The design and colours were timeless and she would never change it if avoidable.

She ascended the stairs and wandered through rooms as she had last evening until she was able to enter the striking and brilliant kitchen that had been off bounds last evening. Sally was pounding her fist into a mound of dough but otherwise the room was brilliantly clean. "Sorry to interrupt, but I am looking for Jennifer."

Sally looked up and brushed away the few wisps of hair, that had escaped her barely visible hairnet. She may not be in a restaurant kitchen with strict health codes, but darned if simple and smart procedures of cleanliness would be relaxed when she worked. "No problem, good to see you wandering around." The comment was delivered with a genuine smile, so no misread snide interpretation. "I am just setting up my dough for fresh baking in the morning. Bread and buns do not last with the men in this house."

"I hope I am still here for a sample tomorrow. I have not had homemade bread since leaving Albany. My mum only makes it on special occasions now, but it still makes my mouth water with the thought." Betty could almost taste her mum's cinnamon buns.

"I will make sure the hounds leave you a crumb or two." Happy to have the threat of bimbo in their midst removed with this lovely and seemingly wholesome lady. Then pointing with her elbow. "That door opens to the basement. The security offices are below and Jennifer will be easy to find as they are open spaces."

"Oh, thanks again for the excellent meals and I hope this was not too stressful on yourself and the team today. I was just following David's requests. I will be going home tomorrow, as like you, have a job to get back to." Betty smiled with her thanks and grateful to have the smiles returned before heading down another flight of stairs in search of Jennifer.

Chapter 10

Betty entered the stairwell to the basement and noticed that it was wired in a similar fashion as the laundry room she had entered with David on Friday evening. The overhead lighting was instant, crisp and brilliant. She was expecting a small landing, but instead was amazed to see what appeared to have been expanded to serve as a mudroom with an exit to the outside. The walls, were a sand colour with dark wood open locker style cubbies for each staff member. The 6 lockers each, had a top shelf for hats, the middle contained 3 hooks each for sweaters and jackets, the bottom was a bench at chair height with 2 shelves below each for footwear. It was relatively easy to determine some of the ownership.

Sally's cubbie had cloth shopping bags and an assortment of pashmina scarves for the evening and several pairs of dress sandals. Arlo's contained work boots, gloves and straw hats. The three-security members had, dress jackets and highly polished sturdy police shoes, Jennifer's were smaller so much easier to identify, plus she had a pair of black 1-inch heels for dressier occasions when the oxfords would not be appropriate with wearing a dress. Pirro's had, tennis shoes, a sewing basket, cleaning caddy and a bag of rags to be used as cleaning cloths. Betty found this strange, that Pirro would keep her cleaning supplies there, but then this was not her home.

What Betty did consider as she descended another stairwell, that this was not some old rickety basement set of stairs. The stairwell width had been expanded to be very wide as Betty could almost stretch her arms out fully at her sides. The riser for the steps had been rebuilt with the expansion obvious from the omission of old boards groaning with the weight of a step. Instead of, bare wood the step treads were covered in a non-slip material that Betty had only seen on the washroom floors of high-end spa facilities. As she moved down the stairs, another recessed ceiling pot light illuminated, erasing any concern of a missed step.

Betty reached the basement and noted the same flooring continued allowing her to step into an open area containing a large glass conference table with eight office chairs. The outside wall to her left contained a large TV type screen panel, 2 large white boards and 1 large corkboard. At the far end of the open space was a glass walled off gym area that at a glance appeared to contain the latest in fitness equipment. To the right of the open area were 3 large open area offices, while wide they were no more than 8-feet in depth. Given the footprint of the house above, Betty figured the house was either built with a half basement, or there was more behind the office areas.

Sally had been correct in saying that Jennifer would be easy to find. The lights had indicated to both Jennifer and Josh that someone was heading down the stairs and when Jennifer recognised her yoga outfit felt there was not need to call out and startle the poor woman. She let Betty take in the workspace and then called out from her middle office space.

"Over here in the middle, grab a chair from the table and have a seat with me at my desk."

Betty pulled a rolling chair from the conference table and was intending to place herself opposite Jennifer. Jennifer was moving a few stacks of books on her desk to a tall filing credenza, on the back wall of her office space and then reached over to pull the chair from around front to be at the end of the desk. She then moved her computer screen so that Betty would have full view. "We have had some time to review the security tapes and do some preliminary searches with your information. I want to bring you up to speed and ensure we are on the right track." Jennifer was all business, treating Betty like a co-worker rather than a houseguest.

Betty took a seat and adjusted herself to have a full view of Jennifer's screen. She then held out her hand to show a plain black device. "I really need to charge my phone, not sure if you have a charger that will work." Betty was holding out her iPhone to Jennifer.

Jennifer pulled a cord from the side of her desk, took the phone from Betty's hand and connected the device to begin charging. "Perfect, it's the same model as mine. We have an assortment of chargers from old phones, but first try is a match. I see it is turned off from running out of battery, so let's leave it off for now."

Betty was a little taken back by this comment. "I will likely have messages from friends and family that will be looking for me. My friend Julia will be expecting an update from the party."

"I get that, but we need to review what may be happening here so that you understand how this could be a huge security risk for David. I do not want you telling anyone you are here until we fully understand what we are dealing with. Can you give us a few more hours? Please!" Jennifer was clearly worried for her boss. This was not just some random incident. It was clearly an intended threat and her job was to ensure the threat was eliminated.

"Ok, but I have no idea how I can help you?" Betty was still puzzled on what more she could add, but after the fear from last evening, she fully understood this was no mistake or accident.

"First of all, we pulled the security footage. This is you entering the front door behind a couple. Can you confirm this is your roommate Kim Barkley and her boyfriend?" Jennifer had adjusted the shot of the three at the entrance and then blown up the picture to zoom in on Kim's face.

"Yes, that is Kim, and her boyfriend Cameron is the man that was in the shot of the three of us." Betty relaxed with the ease of recognition.

"Great dress by the way. Sally, Pirro and I want to know where you got it. Hopefully cleaning will bring it back to how it looked before spending a night on the floor, if not David will replace it." Jennifer spoke so casually that Betty just stared at her.

"I can't remember the name of the store, but am sure I can get the name from the credit card receipt. It is not ripped or stained, just needs a good cleaning and press and it will be fine." Betty looked at the screen now showing back to the three walking in the door. The dress hung wonderfully and Betty saw herself looking very dressed up for the party. The outfit had felt wonderful on Friday night, even her hair pulled back in ponytail suited the look. She had not found a scarf for the ride over, but Cameron had relented and put up the car roof as Kim did not want her own hair messed up.

Jennifer adjusted the zoom again to show a full screen view of only the side of Cameron's face. "This is the boyfriend that you called, Cameron. Are you sure you cannot remember his last name?"

"Sorry, I only know him as Cameron, or sometimes Cam." Betty was sorry she had not shown Kim more interest and asked questions. "To my knowledge he had not been in the condo before Friday night, when I got home from work. He always waited in the car for Kim when he picked her up. It was always so late when she got home, I would have no idea if he walked her to the door or came in. I know he never stayed over if he did come in. Kim did spend nights out with him, occasionally on the weekends, but never during the work week."

"Hum, rather strange behaviour for a boyfriend, or at least I would not like that, but then I am no one to talk about positive relationships until, Arlo." Jennifer had released the zoom back to showing the shot of the three.

Josh appeared at the sidewall and gave Betty a start. "Sorry to startle you, I thought you knew I was working in the next office." He had kind eyes and a wonderful smile that showed his sincerity.

"It's ok, this is all so strange to me, I guess that I am more nervous that I thought." Betty was a little embarrassed that everything was making her jumpy.

"Took Sally over six months to calm down and get comfortable in this house outside of the kitchen. That room she took over in less than an hour. David treats us like extended family, so it is easy for us to be comfortable with all

110

the luxuries we have, but I refuse to become relaxed or complacent in my work." Josh turned his gaze back to Jennifer. "Open that shot I just sent you. I think this is the same couple sitting outside with David."

Jennifer clicked to open the file and her screen filled with a darkened picture of the patio. "This is clear that we need to adjust the camera lighting in the future. Rather dark shot, but it looks like Kim and Cameron. Betty, can you see well enough to confirm?" Jennifer moved her chair over to the wall to allow Betty the opportunity to move closer to the screen.

Betty rose from her chair to get a better look at the darkened image. David had his back to the screen, but even with her recent acquaintance his hair and head shape elegantly placed on those now unmistakable shoulders made a positive identification. The view of Kim was a little grainy in the darkened frame, allowing Betty to rely on hairstyle, jewellery, outfit and shoes to confirm a positive. Betty looked over at the simple styling of Jennifer's hair and smiled.

"I have never figured out how Kim manages to keep that hair so perfect. It is definitely her hair. The outfit and shoes I recognise from Kim's shopping purchase, the day the party invitations arrived, that was draped over our sofa. I had to endure 2-hours of detailed shopping techniques. The jewellery was new and a gift from Cameron that evening, which Kim was only too happy to shove in my face before getting into the car. It was also the topic of conversation by Kim on the 20-minute drive here."

Jennifer laughed out loud with Betty's review. "You may want to think about having a comedy act. Your sense of humour is very dry, but I really like it." Jennifer smiled at Betty with the genuine compliment. "So, we have David and

Kim but again the man is in a profile position for the camera." Jennifer was beginning to think this guy was intentionally avoiding camera shots. So, he clearly knew to spot a camera.

"Well, that one is easy as well. I would recognise that linen suit, expensive loafers with no socks and I know of no man, that is not gay that wears a thick gold chain necklace. Good grief that look went out in the '90s." Betty suddenly realised that her summation of Cameron was tainted with her clear distaste for the man.

This time, not only was Jennifer laughing out loud, but Josh was leaned over the desk for another view of the screen and was laughing equally as hard as Jennifer. "Ok, clearly you have identified Cameron and when this case is over, we are entering you in amateur comedy night at our favourite bar."

Josh stood back up to his full height and was nodding in agreement with Jennifer. Still smiling with the remaining laughter in his eyes he turned to Betty. "With your identification, we can replay this footage and see if there is a shot anywhere on the tape that shows is face full on. Then we can run it through Naldo's program to return identification. It will work with the profile but best to feed it a full view of the guy." Josh moved back to his own desk and could be heard working at his computer.

Jennifer turned to Betty. "I will get you another outfit for tomorrow. Would you prefer a skirt and blouse, or more yoga wear?"

"Uh… thanks. A skirt would be nice, then I can wear my own shoes to go home." Betty was still getting used to all the generosity.

Jennifer stood and opened a panel behind her desk. It revealed a cosy sitting room with another room, beyond which Jennifer continued through. She returned quickly to the office space with a skirt and blouse on a hanger and closed the panel door. "I do not have many of these outfits as I only wear them off duty, but Pirro thought this would suit your colours the best. Your underwear is being laundered and Pirro will have it in your room by morning so no need for more of mine."

Betty looked at the simple patterned skirt and solid coloured blouse smiling at Jennifer in approval. "Thanks so much, I will have it cleaned and returned on Monday. Do you live here?" Indicating to the panel door Jennifer had used.

"Yup, we all do. Josh and Sally have the suite behind his office and the same with Naldo and Pirro next door. I was the last on the team so got the middle office, but matters little to me. They are all the same size and the same comforts, so no issue. Everyone uses the gym equipment including, David. Sally keeps us all fed, Pirro cares for the interior of the house and all laundry and Arlo cares for the exterior of the house." Jennifer summed it up so simply.

"That is really nice, but don't you step on each other? Family is one thing but this is people working and living together." Betty was puzzled by the simplicity Jennifer was providing.

"As Security, we are often only here during the early morning and evening, then we accompany David as singles or pairs, as needed. I was mainly brought on to be with his mother, when his parents are in residence. If he ever has a date or an escort, I am there for the female and often I act as his escort to events, as David is not much for dates. Arlo was already working these grounds through his family business, so when we married, this and the adjoining properties became his only focus."

"Pirro cares for this house and, similar to Arlo, the adjoining properties as well. Friday was an exception to bring in caterers, as Sally generally does everything food and drink related, and even on Friday she was in charge. She even makes meals for the neighbours when they are here, which is not very often anymore. We are all very busy during the day, and in the evening, we have the house space to use plus the outside and when we want privacy, we each have a sitting room." Jennifer again stuck with the simplicity.

"What about your own families? Don't you ever want to have a family of your own?" Betty was still puzzled, but the cleaning kit in the back entry now made sense, with Pirro caring for the neighbouring homes. However, she did not see this simple situation lasting very long with young couples.

"Josh was an army brat and his parents retired to Montana on a ranch. Sally's family never supported her being a Chef. They were fine when she was taking classes in Europe, but when she came back to the states and worked for a restaurant in Miami, it was the last straw. They are some old-money family in New York and did not even attend their wedding. Naldo and Pirro are from Cuban immigrant families, as is Arlo."

"Much of their families are still in the Miami area and they go to visit often, but neither let on how well they are doing to best anyone else they love. Arlo's family does not approve of me so we are on our own. We have made a family in this home." Jennifer was clearly holding back when she spoke of Arlo and herself. It was obvious how she provided details on the others but not on herself.

Betty picked up on this unwillingness to talk about herself so went back to the original question. "So that explains how you live together and why, but it does not address eventually having a family of your own. Or are you not interested in children?"

"Oh no, we are all very interested. The two houses we care for are owned by couples in their 80s. Their families do not like them here alone and for some reason don't want to spend too much time here either. David has asked both to give him right of first refusal when they are ready to sell their properties. The idea is, then we would have more space for our own families as they come along. If babies happen before the neighbours are ready to sell, David has invited us to move upstairs."

"I am personally not in a hurry to have a baby, so it is not an issue for us, but Pirro has been talking about it very openly for the past few months. It would not be a surprise to have an announcement from them soon. Not really sure about the timing for Sally, she did not have a great childhood, thus she is very slow to make a move. Josh on the other hand, wants to have his own soccer team so could be interesting for them." Jennifer was sharing more and more with Betty. It was hard not to be friendly with such another open person.

Betty was just about to continue with more questioning when Josh popped around the corner again. "Got something, can you please come and verify?" He was looking straight at Betty to further clarify that it was her confirmation required.

Betty and Jennifer moved to Josh's area and there on the screen was what appeared to be a driver's license photo of

Cameron. "How did you get that information?" Betty was truly taken aback by this personal information appearing on Josh's computer.

"I still have great contacts with the Police department. David had to sign off on our use of this information for security threats only. Believe me, I will be writing a report to support this search. We do not do this on a whim." Jennifer was trying to be clear enough to avoid further questions but not so.

"So, you took a picture of me this morning on the deck with David and ran my photo as well?" Betty was staring at Jennifer for an answer.

"Yes, we did. David has never stayed holed up in his room like that before. Honestly, it gave all of us a scare." It was Josh that responded to Betty's question directed at Jennifer. He was the team leader and would stand by his decision.

Betty moved her stare to Josh and then relaxed. Given the same circumstance she would have reacted equally. "I get it." Then Betty thought of the results of the search. "So, what came back on me?"

"Took us longer to get your information as you still have a New York State license. You have never had a traffic violation, never had an accident, nothing. How have you been driving since, 16 years of age and not a single incident?" Josh had never seen a clean profile unless the person had only been driving under a month. His own record was not that clean.

"I really don't drive too much, but when I do, I follow the rules." Betty saw the simplicity of her statement. She did not understand what an anomaly she was.

"Well, I like to think that I follow the rules as well, but you are amazing, and can borrow my car anytime." Josh

116

thought of the minor scratches and dings that Sally would have no idea how they happened. He could never own a new vehicle; it was not worth the pain of Sally driving away and knowing it would not come back the same as leaving.

Betty just smiled at the compliment. Peter and her parents had never cared if she asked for their vehicles; perhaps it was always driving someone else's car that had caused her to be so cautious. Getting her own when she returned home, should receive the same care, as if borrowed from another, yet more because it would be all hers.

Jennifer had been happy that Josh stepped up to the question of running Betty this morning. She had been against the action, but as team leader Josh had overridden her concern. "Let's get back on task." Jennifer was anxious to get on with identifying Cameron she was tired and really hoping this would not drag into an all-nighter.

Again, Betty found herself leaning over to get a clear look at the picture. She did not want to make a false identification on some poor guy. "Well, it certainly looks like Cameron, but the clincher is that trashy chain."

Jennifer and Josh looked closer at the screen themselves and then laughed.

"You have a cop's eye for detail. I am so happy to have you helping." Jennifer had missed the chain, so was impressed. That was her second miss in 24 hours!

"Detail is everything in my work. I could never do the work of a police officer." Betty was convinced after last night, that detective work was not her calling.

"I will disagree as you protected David last night better than we did!" Jennifer was still feeling ashamed, for not having been watching David more closely. She had been feeling horrible last night and was clearly not on her game.

"All I did was help him up the stairs and do a few Google searches on my phone. The rest was play-acting on his insistence. I wanted to call 911 and bolt from this house." Betty still just wanted to go home and leave everything to the Security team.

"We appreciate you staying and the identification. This gives us enough to work with and have a report in the morning. Jennifer will walk you back to your room and make sure you have all that you need for a good rest." Josh nodded to Jennifer as a signal to take Betty back upstairs and returned to his investigation, on who this Cameron was and how it related to David.

Chapter 11

Jennifer and Betty arrived back in the kitchen with the loaned outfit and Betty's phone remained on Jennifer's desk. While the household had expanded their trust of Betty, they did not want Betty falling into the easy habit of checking for messages or emails.

The kitchen was filled with Sally, Pirro, Naldo and Arlo. All were sitting comfortably at the large island enjoying assorted drinks and a plate of baking. Sally popped up with the arrival of two more. "Can I get you both something?"

Jennifer looked at Betty. "Would you like a snack before turning in? Sally always has hot and cold drinks at the ready."

Betty nodded a no to Jennifer. "I should go up and check on David and make sure he is resting comfortably before turning in."

The others seated at the island shared smiles and raised eyebrows before Pirro spoke up. "I just came down from checking on David. He finished the tea and cookies that Sally took up earlier. He's out cold and did not even move when I checked his forehead for a fever."

"Well, that is a relief." Betty commented with a sigh. "Thank you, Sally, that is very kind, but I did not sleep well last evening so will just turn in myself." She turned to Jennifer to take the hanger of clothing. "I can find my way up, unless it is part of your job to see me to my room?"

Jennifer smiled and released the hanger. "I will just do one more check of the front door and windows. Just pick up the phone beside your bed and it will ring in the kitchen if you need anything."

Betty thought of her phone on Jennifer's desk. "Are you not concerned of me calling from the landline?"

Naldo laughed this time. "Nope, that phone only connects to the kitchen."

The flush of embarrassment returned to Betty's cheeks. It was clear their trust of her only extended so far. "Well… good night, all." Betty left the kitchen with her limited dignity and fresh clothing for the next day.

Jennifer returned to the group in the kitchen, following her check of the main floor. She had lingered to hear Betty's movement on the second floor and noted the hesitation from the hallway looking into David's room. While David and his family rarely closed doors to their room's day or night, Jennifer noted the soft click and turn of the lock of Betty's room for the evening.

It had been the closed and locked doors to David's area that had alerted the team during the party and then in the morning. The concern of trust from David over the last 24 hours was being discussed in the kitchen, but Jennifer wanted to remain focused on all the facts and how to mitigate rather than engage in whining.

"Come on Naldo, we have a confirmed ID and need to finish our report for the morning. We all know David will be expecting answers. The other stuff can be addressed later."

Jennifer headed for the basement stairs, with Naldo following closely.

Sally watched their exit from the kitchen then turned her attention to Arlo. "Is Jennifer, ok? She hardly ate today, and this is the first time she passed up a snack before going down."

"Might be some flu, she has been tired even in the morning after a long sleep." Arlo had not noticed the eating change, just as Sally did. But being tired was new for Jennifer. She was always first up and, in the gym, endless energy during the day and evenings, and plenty left for him regardless of the busy day with David. Once this issue was sorted out, they could talk and he would drag her to a doctor if necessary. The girls would help with that for sure.

What Arlo missed when wrapped in his own thoughts, was the shared look between the other women. Pirro was generally quiet and not one to force an opinion but this evening she spoke very clearly to Arlo. "She needs to see a doctor and Monday if possible. I hope it is only the flu, but what if it is something more?"

Arlo was startled by this comment. His mind raced to all horrible health issues. "Oh my God in heaven, do you think I need to take her into the hospital tonight?"

The look of fear in Arlo's eyes was very real and Pirro was immediately ashamed of her off-hand comment. "No Arlo, I do not think it is that serious. I just think you need to ensure she gets a check-up soon. We don't need a flu in this house taking us all down."

Sally backed Pirro up. "Agreed, I for one cannot have you all sniffling and coughing in my kitchen. And on that note, we all need to get some rest after a late night yesterday and with so many questions for what is going on, we may all have extra tasks tomorrow." Sally began clearing the dishes while the others helped. It was not enough to just wipe down counters, they had to be cleaned with disinfectant. This was not a restaurant requirement, but the standards for cleaning for Sally were higher.

The three spouses entered the common area of the basement, to find their partners using the boardroom table and big screen, instead of individual computers. Each offered assistance to their mate and then just a kiss good night, before retreating to their individual suites. The three-security team would not rest until a report was prepared for David.

Chapter 12

Sunday morning, Betty woke to a wonderful warm light filling her very spacious room. Not wanting to say that her room at the condo wasn't lovely, but this was decadence. It was like being in a fancy hotel suite including all the bath luxuries. This room was done in wonderful light peach silks, for the bedding and window treatments. The walls a soft blue with all of the furniture brilliant glossy white. The attached bathroom continued the peach theme with peach walls and the marble had a peach vein. The floors and cabinets again were brilliant white, but the best being paintings of beach meeting the ocean in calm waves that made Betty feel she could touch it. One scene, was of day with sunlight twinkling off the sand and water, and the other of, evening showing all the beautiful oranges and reds of the sunsets that she would miss back in Albany. Betty was unable to decipher the artist's signature, so made a mental note to ask David. She would need to acquire something similar for her new home back in Albany, just to bring the memory home.

But there was a task to be completed, and she has been absent from her life long enough. She will be very firm this morning and demand to have her phone, to return messages. Both Julie and her parents, were likely frantic by now and

Betty had no intention of dragging them into this scenario. Plus, if David wanted to avoid the police being involved, having a search of her whereabouts would not be in his best interest.

Not giving herself the time for a soak in the lovely marble tub, smaller than David's, she did enjoy the shower and all the toiletries laid out by Pirro, for her use. The borrowed skirt and blouse from Jennifer fit perfectly, her own undergarments and shoes boosted her spirit and confidence as she gathered her handbag and stepped from the guest room.

This morning as Betty ascended the stairs, she was able to truly appreciate the blending of the stained glass colours as the sunlight pierced through the glass dome. The reflection drew her eye, to the inlaid gleam imbedded in the railing. Now, in the light, she was able to appreciate the highly polished smoky quartz. Her friend Julia, loved crystals and been keen to learn all about their healing properties and proper usage. As a result, Betty was well aware that smoky quartz was known for its grounding properties and natural clearing of negativity.

Rather fitting and a comfort considering the serious situation. Betty held her hand over a portion of the railing, ensuring to touch the crystal, intending to gather strength and clarity for the day ahead. The warmth and colours piercing through the glass dome above, surrounded her as she paused to take a few cleansing breaths, as the Albany counsellor had instructed, and prayed to God, that she would come out of this situation whole and return to her very boring life.

Betty realised within herself, that while she was able to deal with the stress of the situation clearly on Friday night, it was not an experience she cared to encounter often, as was the case for Jennifer and the security team. Betty intended to keep her attention to detail focused on software products and successful implementation.

Instead of heading for the kitchen, Betty followed the voices and sound of dishes being placed into a large and very formal dining room. Had Betty continued her exit from the house on Friday night, she would have walked by this room, instead she had stopped in the hallway, in search of a bathroom and encountered David, which changed everything.

The room, while formal in appearance, was clearly being used otherwise. The house habitants were laying place settings for everyone, herself included, with the count. Platters of breakfast food items were being placed in the middle of the table, to be passed around like any family dinner. Sweating jugs of water and juice had already been set and Sally entered from another doorway holding two carafes.

"Coffee is hot and ready. Betty, great to see you found us, we were going to come and ask you to join us." Sally spoke naturally, as she set a carafe at each end of the table.

David rose from his chair with Sally's announcement. "Please join us, the team has a plan and Josh feels you can be a key part of it." He held out his hand as a gesture for Betty to take it, and pulled the chair beside him, from the table for her to be seated.

The growling in Betty's tummy and the scent of coffee were too big of a pull, to walk away. She approached the waiting chair, but avoided David's hand. It would be so easy to accept the warmth and intimacy of his touch, but she knew it was just manners and not the gesture of a welcoming love, wanting continual physical contact.

Following the awkward seating of Betty and many exchanged glances by the others, David seated himself and immediately bowed his head as did the others. "Heavenly Father, we offer thanks for this food, and the blessings of this household. In Jesus' name, Amen."

Betty watched the reaction from the others. Not that she was overly religious, and not a regular church attender, but like her own family, fully believe in God and the value of giving thanks and gratitude. It was obviously common in this house as well, adding another layer of comfort to her being part of this situation.

The platters of food were passed around allowing each to take what they wanted for volume, the women were more select in their portions, while the men heaped on food like a starving soul's void of sustenance. David was cautious in his selections and Betty was concerned he was still feeling the ill effects of the Jimsonweed. "Are you feeling, ok?" She asked David in a whisper.

"A little tired still, but this is my second breakfast." David admitted with a sheepish look. "I woke up early starving, so Sally made me a poached egg and toasted a slice of her bread, as it came from the oven. I am heeding your advice to be cautious."

The satisfying sounds of enjoyment from the first bites relaxed Betty further into the sharing of this family meal. As mouths were emptied of food, the compliments to Sally were lavishly extolled. Sally blushed and waved them off not wanting a fuss. It made Betty happy to see that contributions to this household-team were appreciated.

Following a few satisfying bites, Josh began his summary of their investigation. "Thanks to Betty we have been able to identify both her roommate, Kimberly Barkley, Kim, and her boyfriend, Cameron Lauther. Reviewing the security tapes, we have confirmed David's belief that it was the pineapple as the source of his poisoning. The tapes show Cameron putting something on two of the plates and then being very careful not to give one of the tainted plates to Kim. We all know how David loves a pineapple, so not a big surprise, that he gobbled his up quickly, but it is very clear that Cameron did not touch his, he did not want to be poisoned."

Naldo set down his utensils and picked up the story. "My investigation revealed that Cameron is the son of, Samuel Lauther. Samuel is the owner of Gainesville Enterprises. A company that started in Gainesville, Florida, as a construction company and moved into pipeline building. As he became more successful, Samuel expanded to purchasing pipelines and the ownership of their small companies. He then began to acquire trucking companies with the intention of forming a major oil and gas midstream presence."

"For anyone that does not know that term, it is the middle process. Oil and gas are broken into three business components, upstream, midstream and downstream. Upstream is the search and extraction of products. Downstream is the refining, marketing and distribution of products, like gasoline for our cars. Midstream is the movement of products from say, an oil well to the refinery. Rail and tanker shipping are also part of midstream and my research shows that, Mr Lauther is working on acquiring those areas as well. But what is currently missing in the pipeline area is David's company."

"Thank you both for the great summary." David nodded to both men. "What is absent from your research is that

Gainesville Enterprises approached me some time ago for a purchase, which I declined. Lauther has approached me several times since, also continuously declined. The second, and following Friday night, I am thinking may be related to my declining these offers, is that I have been asked to appear this week in the office for a review audit of my business practices by the Florida Department of Environmental Protection."

"There has been no information to support this review, only that if my presence is not at this meeting, I will forfeit my current operating permit. Naldo believes that Cameron, through Kim has been looking for a weakness in our organisation for some months, and his poisoning on Friday was to ensure I was not able to personally attend the meeting scheduled tomorrow."

Betty reached for David's hand. She had no idea business could be this cut throat! She had heard of ruthless business dealings, after all she lived in the State of New York where, Wall Street was constantly in the press. Apparently, business was business everywhere and here in Miami was no exception.

David had felt her take his hand before he finished speaking and was comforted by the gesture. He turned his attention to her specifically and openly addressed her with a shimmer of tears in his eyes. "Betty, I owe you everything for your care and identification of the poison on Friday. And to the rest of you, this is yet another open and formal apology, that I ever doubted you or your professional dedication. I ask each of you to accept my apology for not calling you in that night, but if you still feel slighted by my lack of trust on

Friday, I will fully understand." David had moved his gaze from Betty to engage each of his staff separately.

The team at the table all started to speak at once. They all accepted his apology, confirming no one had any intention of leaving his employ. Josh, being the lead, summed it up for everyone. "Just don't ever to that again! We are a team!"

The agreement and comments of concern continued for another few minutes until, David brought them back into focus. "Now that we know the issue, Jennifer has a great plan to respond to Lauther. Jennifer, can you please explain to the rest and their roles."

"Ok, we have created a plan that is workable, but Betty, we need you to be the main player." Jennifer directed her look to Betty.

"Me? What can I offer?" Betty just wanted to go home and put this weekend behind her.

"You are the best access to Kim we have. We have set up a plan for me to come home with you, and you to go to work this week as normal. Could you stick with us a few more days?" Jennifer was trying to get her to agree, but did not want to reveal the full plan without agreement.

David took Betty's hand again and looked directly into her eyes. "Please help us, you are the best plan we have."

Betty looked back at his eyes. "First, we agreed that no more puppy looks. Second, I am not cut out for this type of intrigue. That being said, I would like to see this through, so if it is simple enough, and does not cause me to be physically in danger then yes. But I need to contact my family and friends. I have been out of contact since Friday and they will be getting nervous." Betty had turned to look at Jennifer.

Jennifer pulled a phone from her pocket. "This is yours, and it is fully charged. I would like to be with you when you contact them, and use text messages to avoid a conversation if possible. How you respond to them is also based on our plan to provide a complete cover story, but we need your agreement first." Jennifer handed the phone to Betty.

Betty took the phone from Jennifer and pressed the power button to turn it on and sign in to ensure it was actually hers. She remembered that Jennifer's was the same. As the device finished its power up process, notification sounds relayed the signal of several missed messages of varying types. Betty looks at the front screen. "I have 3 missed calls and 8 text messages, plus several emails. I guess we better get this plan laid out, so I can respond. I'm in." Betty took a, huge, deep breath to finish her statement of agreement.

Naldo started the overview of the plan. "I did not hack your phone or email account, but I did troll your Facebook page. You have a cousin in California that loves herself a lot, and wants to appear younger than she is. She appears to be on a 4-week European cruise that we can use to our benefit. My proposal, is to use her absence as not really being on a cruise, but instead having cosmetic surgery here in Miami. Things did not go as smoothly as intended and you received a call to go to the clinic on Friday night. You have been with her at the clinic all weekend and Jennifer will pose as your cousin to bring back to your place to recover in secret."

"I have not seen my cousin for over ten years. My mother rarely talks to her sister, as they lead such a different life than my parents. The cover could actually work, but I think it best if I do not reveal the name of the person needing my help on Friday to my mum. If I tell my mum, it is my cousin, she will call her sister. I will just say it is someone in our condo building that needed my help. But to Kim, I could draw her into my confidence by saying it is my cousin. As her name is also Jennifer, we can likely make this work. By the way, what did you have done?" Betty smiled as she looked questionably at Jennifer.

"I was thinking a boob job or tummy tuck would be a good cover. Arlo, which do you prefer?" Jennifer askes her husband jokingly.

"I would prefer neither actually, but if we have to pick one, let's go with boobs, can't get enough of those." Arlo hugged his wife with the joke.

"Ok, what you are wearing will get us to your house, but I need a travel suitcase. Pirro and Sally, I can get you to scan the pictures on Cousin Jennifer's Facebook and fill a travel case with clothing, shoes, intimates and cosmetics." Pirro and Sally nod acceptance of the shopping challenge.

"Arlo will be using his gardening truck stationed around your neighbourhood as surveillance and Naldo will be going into the office today to do a computer security check. He will put a recording device on Kim's phone and computer to monitor, but we will not be able to get close enough to clone her cell phone. We are thinking, that she is only a patsy in all of this, but need to be sure and also ensure there is no other leak in the company. Josh will stay with David at all times, when outside of this house. This covers all our concerns, Betty, we want you to stick to your routine as much as possible, other than caring for your cousin." Jennifer sits back to sip her coffee feeling good about the plan.

More details were discussed while breakfast was finished, as well as plans for the remainder of the morning. The group dispersed with their assignments and David returned to his room for a nap. It was clear to all, that while his appetite was great, his strength would take some time to recover and he needed to look strong at the office, the next day.

Jennifer sat with Betty in her basement office space for the remainder of the morning. Betty returned all messages from her parents and Julie using text/email and Jennifer showed her how to leave a phone message, so as to appear as a call had been missed by the receiving party. She noted in all messages, that phone calls were not allowed in the private hospital, so texting was best. Her parents were relieved to hear that Betty was fine, but Julie was a tougher nut. Julie wanted details from the party and was scolding Betty for running to the aid of her narcissistic cousin. Betty had a good laugh and could hardly wait to tell Julie the actual truth, including every detail with Mr David Baffa.

Chapter 13

Betty and Jennifer arrived back at her condo by taxi in the late afternoon of Sunday. Betty was carrying a plain white plastic bag from a local deli, Jennifer's Chanel tote and her own small party purse. The cab driver popped the trunk, to extract Jennifer's bags and a plain plastic bag containing Betty's beautiful party dress. Sally and Pirro had thoroughly enjoyed shopping and were surprised that David had not even winced at the receipts. Sally had used the house credit card and spent more in one day than she normally did for a year of groceries and household items.

In actuality, when David skimmed over the receipts from Sally, he internally noted that his own mother spent more on a single shopping trip, and she did this on a regular basis. Plus, he enjoyed hearing the ladies discuss how they would share the special items, once the ordeal was over. David knew he paid well and treated his staff as family, but to be able to provide an extra perk was truly fun.

Betty helped Jennifer from the car and added a generous tip, asking the driver to carry the matching Louis Vuitton rolling case and cosmetics case up the stairs to front door. The driver completed a second trip to relieve Betty of her bags and after ensuring the ladies were progressing well but gingerly, raced off to his next fare. He had picked up this fare at the lobby of a known private clinic in an office building, so the driver was sure some major work had been completed for the one lady requiring assistance.

Betty opened the condo door with her key and started the conversation script. "These deli items will get us through tonight and tomorrow breakfast. I will get groceries on my way home from work so that you can have home cooked meals and soup to help you recover."

Jennifer grabbed Betty's hand and her own tote in a startled act. "You did not tell me you have a man living here!"

Betty had been assisting Jennifer through the door and turned to see Cameron approaching. "Sorry to scare you, I am Cameron. Betty, you help your friend in and I will get the bags." Cameron had extended his hand as a gesture of greeting but Jennifer had sincerely hoped for this scenario and had responded as planned by shying away from Cameron's welcome.

Jennifer continued to act a little frightened and with Betty's assistance they passed through the living area to Betty's bedroom. Kim had jumped off the couch at seeing Jennifer and reached to take the deli and Chanel bag from both. Jennifer clutched possessively at the tote handle and Betty gave Kim a rolling her eyes look releasing only the deli bag. "I will put this in the kitchen for you." Kim smiled weakly at Jennifer and Betty.

Cameron brought the luggage and the sad dress bag into Betty's bedroom with a quick exit. Jennifer was actually whimpering, with tears streaking her heavy makeup as Betty helped her to the bed. "You just lay down for a bit and gather yourself. I am going to make you a cup of tea." Betty said clearly, as Cameron and Kim are standing just outside of the bedroom.

Jennifer whimpered more in agreement and with all kinds of wonderful sounds of pain and exertion to settle herself on Betty's bed. Old Mr Bains, from drama would have been so proud of Jennifer.

"I will be just in the kitchen making tea if you need me, I will hear your call." Jennifer smiled knowingly at Betty, allowing her to exit the room and close the door.

In the kitchen, Betty set the kettle, made Jennifer a cup of tea and refrigerate the deli items. Kim had just plunked the bag on the kitchen counter but was back in a flash offering to help. Even Cameron stood at the nook counter ensuring they had enough supplies. "I would be happy to run out and get anything more, after all I have car and know you girls don't."

Betty was so thankful that her head was shielded by the fridge door placing items on shelves at this comment, or her expression would have likely blown the whole caper. Instead, she popped back up and sincerely addressed Cameron. "That is so thoughtful Cameron, but I am sure we have lots until I can shop tomorrow."

"So, who is she? And where have you been all weekend? We have not seen you since arriving at the party on Friday, and when we left, we looked for you everywhere but you were gone. Not even Jeremy knew where you went." Kim was in rapid-fire question mode and did not even give Betty a chance to answer questions.

Betty waited until Kim stopped talking and then started another planned speech. "Well first, she is my cousin, Jennifer, from California. I have been with her all weekend. She told everyone in her family that she was going on a

European cruise and instead booked herself into a private surgery here in Miami. Things did not go well, because she was taking some undisclosed diet pill that caused an adverse reaction to the sedation medication. The clinic called me at the party Friday night and I grabbed a cab right away. I have been at the clinic with her all weekend. She would not even let me call my Auntie."

Betty added a few sniffles and let her tears form up a bit to enhance the drama factor. "I found a nearby shop for some clothing but think my other dress is ruined. To top it off, she will likely need to be here for the entire week until she is cleared to fly back to Los Angeles." Betty saw the look from Kim at the mention of her dress.

"I will send your dress to my cleaners with explicit instructions. It did look really good on you, not my style obviously, but no sense in having it destroyed. But if Jennifer is staying in your room, where will you sleep? Perhaps I should stay with you this week Cameron." Kim turned to him with the last statement.

Cameron covered quickly. "My place is a mess, plus you should stay here with Betty in case she needs any help with her cousin."

Betty looked longingly at the couch where the couple had been sitting, as practiced repeatedly with Jennifer, and quietly said. "Well... I was hoping to have the couch, that would be better than trying to sleep in the clinic chairs as I did all weekend."

Cameron jumps on this suggestion. "Well, if you are sure, you do not need anything, Kim we should go out for a nice dinner and let Betty get some rest." Kim was happy to be going out for dinner, the deli food Betty picked up looked very unappealing. She was still disappointed there was not an offer for her to spend the entire week at Cameron's place.

Betty continued with preparing tea for Jennifer as the couple left. Betty also noted that Cameron was driving a dark sedan rather than his flashy sports car. No wonder, she did not pick up on him being in the condo when they arrived. Jennifer had hoped and planned for Cameron to be at the condo but with not recognising the car on arrival, Betty had thought Jennifer was wrong.

She took the tea into the bedroom and immediately Jennifer placed a finger to her lips to indicate no talking. Instead, Jennifer talked. "Betty thanks for the tea, just set it beside me. Can you help me up to the powder room?" No please, just an expectation of assistance.

Betty stood, confused as Jennifer got up and slowly with plenty of groans and moans and made her way to the bathroom, indicating for Betty to follow. Jennifer closed the bathroom door and continued to make whimpering noises of painful effort, while she used the toilet.

With the toilet flushing and the sink water running Jennifer whispered. "I swept your room for bugs and found one. I will sweep the common area after it is dark. Sound only in your room, no camera, so we have to be careful in our communication, even if they are out of the unit. We can use hand signals in your bedroom and lots of notes that we can burn with the cover of scented candles." Jennifer was rattling off information in her professional manner. Much of what she had found, was expected by her team.

"What the hell!" This was more than Betty was prepared for. "You said this might happen but I cannot believe that Cameron was in my room and Kim let him!"

"It is highly likely that Kim knows nothing. I am getting the impression she does not. He probably waited until she used the bathroom herself or something, which is why there is no camera, not the required time to set one up. Gotta love Naldo and his gadgets, the bug is behind the picture of your parents, by the way."

"Great! Well, if Your Highness does not need anything else, I am going to make up the couch and get some sleep before work tomorrow. Or are you going to whine all night?" Betty was trying to make light of the situation even if it was rather unnerving.

"I am thinking I will drink my tea while you get settled on the couch, then ask you for some food to take my pain meds and finally conk out around nine." Jennifer was enjoying the simplicity of this plan and also looking forward to the added rest it would naturally allow. She had been feeling rather tired lately and had attributed it to the preparation of the house party.

"Well let's get you back to bed." Betty turns off the water so the last sentence may be heard. And the two slowly return to the bed to get Jennifer settled and followed the plan for the evening. Just enough talking, to add credibility to the care required for breast surgery. Sally and Pirro had researched the procedure and shopped as if, Sally was to be the recipient. The health aid store carrying the necessary equipment were familiar with the procedure by many firms in the Miami area. Naldo had fabricated appropriate pain medication labels and containers filled with generic vitamin supplements.

Betty used the spare bedding in her closet to make up the couch. Then wrote out a note for Jamel and placed it on the kitchen counter. Jennifer had suggested leaving the note where Kim and Cameron could read it, but they all hoped that Cameron would not re-enter the unit until Jennifer had flown back to California. With the planted listening devise, there was really no need, and keeping up the story was essential, to avoid Betty being identified as the woman on the balcony at David's. Naldo was certain that even with a great lens, the distance would be too far, for an accurate match in any facial recognition software.

Betty finally settled around 9:30 p.m. that evening. The routine of caring for Jennifer's surgery took more time than they anticipated but both felt, the recording would be taken as genuine. Exhausted as she was, Betty found herself wide awake and half-expected Kim to come home early.

Instead of rest, her mind drifted back to the scene with David as she and Jennifer prepared to leave his house earlier, in the afternoon. Josh would drive them to the office building and have them enter through the back entrance. Betty would then call a taxi for pick up at the front lobby entrance. The plan was simple and clear, bags were taken to the car and all the staff rushed off to ensure all was in place.

Betty was waiting in the front entry staring up at the colours of the glass ceiling praying she would have the opportunity to see this again and just enjoy the beauty.

"It was the sunlight pouring into the entry with its mixture of colours that captured my heart when looking to purchase a home. I had decided to buy it before I even saw the remaining layout. Thankfully, I had Josh and Sally with me or I would have no idea what the rest even looked like. Sally basically took over all the discussions with the realtor and we even met the neighbours that day." David had approached from behind Betty and was talking very softly.

Rather than being started by his presence, Betty found the snippet of information comforting to know that David valued this space in a similar way to herself. She turned to respond and found herself wrapped up in the strength of his arms. David lowered his mouth to hers and she responded to his kiss with a passion she never knew existed. The kiss was soft yet firm, demanding yet tender. Her mind was spinning off to some other galaxy with a flashing of light behind her closed eyes, that was more brilliant than the colours reflecting through the ceiling. There was a fire forming in her abdomen that was causing her legs to melt like Jell-O left on the counter. She was reaching for the stability of his neck with her right arm when David suddenly broke the contact and took a step back.

Betty almost lost her balance and David secured her stance by holding the underside of her left forearm. The warmth again of his contact calmed her nerves and allowed the remainder of her skeletal structure to regain its strength.

Their eye focus remained fixed on the other and David spoke first. "I thought I heard someone coming and did not want you in a compromised position."

Betty held eye contact but laughed. "A little late for that don't you think? Your entire household had me pegged just slightly higher than a hooker until Saturday afternoon."

David thought for a moment and then laughed himself. "I owe you so much and continue to make a mess of everything. I have honestly never met anyone like you before and find myself tied up in knots. I would like to ask your permission to formally see you when all of this is sorted out. Would you please do me the honour of at least a future dinner?"

The puppy look was back, but the sincerity in his eyes was not just a boy begging for a second cookie, or in his case more pineapple. Betty was not sure he was asking for a date or the opportunity to compensate her for handling a crisis. "How about we focus on getting you healthy and sort out whatever this is, and then we can plan a dinner."

David was about to clarify and say more to define his intent but Josh approached saying everything was in the car waiting for Betty. The three walked to the waiting car and all the household was saying goodbye to both Jennifer and Betty with hugs. They really were a true chosen family. Not one by blood, but one forged through friendship and trust. Arlo had openly kissed Jennifer just before she settled in the car and Betty heard his final comment "Don't forget to make an appointment this week."

Betty thought the comment was strange. Jennifer never forgot a single detail. Part of the plan was a check-up appointment with the clinic on Wednesday. The plan did not call for them to actually see a doctor.

What continued to puzzle Betty as she finally drifted off to sleep was the kiss under the brilliance of the stained-glass light in David's entry.

Chapter 14

Betty got up the next morning and completed her morning routine being extra quiet so as not to wake Jennifer. Jennifer had winked a few times and smiled, but pretended to still be sleeping with the aid of drugs. Betty laid out Jennifer's morning food and was writing a note that she would walk home at lunch to check on her, but to call Betty's cell as needed. Kim was uncharacteristically up and ready for work as well and even offered to help Betty prepare the breakfast tray for Jennifer, and carry it into the bedroom. Betty did not expect this, but Jennifer had, so Betty let her and offered thanks. Kim was being very quiet, but Jennifer pretended to be startled, and screamed, and Kim almost dropped the tray. Then Jennifer started to cry over how much pain she was in, and Kim scurried out the room. Betty was at the door, as if just coming to Kim's aid, and told Kim how sorry she was. She then went in to calm Jennifer and passed a few more notes, prior to leaving. Jennifer was holding a pillow to muffle any laughter. Betty had to take a deep breath of composure, before leaving the bedroom shaking her head in amazement, that this was actually happening.

Betty and Kim walked to work together. Even though this was a rare behaviour, Betty carried on like it happened every day. Kim was chatty the entire time, asking about Jennifer's surgery, which clinic, what happened, when did Betty get the call on Friday night… All the questions Jennifer had prepared Betty to answer without even thinking and therefore to seem very natural.

At the office, Betty grabbed a coffee and settled into her work. Kim was busy socialising about the party, asking everyone what they did, who they talked to, digging for information. Betty appeared to be answering emails, typing away, but in actuality was furiously capturing all the questions and answers, to send to Jennifer and the team.

Around 9:00 a.m. there was another buzz in the office. The company owner, with another man entered and went directly to the boardroom. Jeremy was called in to join them almost immediately and Kim ran to Betty to see if she had been called in as well. Most of the staff did not even know what the owner looked like, even at the party on Friday he was nowhere to be seen. But the office secretary and Kim knew him and were quick to add in confirmation, after Jeremy was called in.

The secretary was then instructed to prepare coffee and snacks for 10:00 a.m. and the buzz started up, that they were expecting additional visitors. Kim was in a flap and so her questions turned to asking about the owner, which Betty was happy to add, she had not previously met the owner. When the second group arrived, everyone in the office became nervous, as no one could identify the second group in dark suits and matching briefcases.

At 10:15 a.m. Betty's cell buzzed, it was Jennifer. She exaggerated a one-sided conversation of Jennifer only being in pain for a few days and the results of such wonderful breasts would all be worth it… Jennifer on the other side was clarifying the data received, and making a few suggestions with the shower running in the background confirming the call in the bathroom.

At 11:05 a.m. her cell buzzed again, Betty had just gathered her team for their scheduled team meeting. Betty rolled her eyes at Kim to indicate that it was Jennifer, again. Kim, on cue, stepped in and offered to cover for Betty – thanks Kim… good grief!

When everyone started to disperse for lunch, Betty gathered her things to head home with a stop at the deli on the way. Kim offered to come and Betty thanked her, but thought, it might be best to be alone as Jennifer was not a good patient. Kim had to agree, following the breakfast tray incident. Betty hurried home with food and spent time for the audio, soothing Jennifer. Jennifer played it up to a point, that Betty was almost happy to go back to work. Betty could not believe how exhausting acting could be and Jennifer smiled and squeezed Betty's hand in recognition of doing great.

Betty noticed a big black SUV when leaving the office an hour ago, she saw it at the deli and again on her way back to work. The third encounter was too much of a coincidence, so Betty snapped a picture of the license plate with her phone, while making it look like she was responding to a message. She emailed the picture to the team and returned to her desk for another round of gossip. Betty was rather thankful that the project was at a stage, that she could have actually offered to leave work for a few days this week and care for Jennifer, but instead gave the appearance of completing project documents.

Kim was doing nothing project related instead, continued talking to everyone and was not even aware of the requirements to wrap up a project. Until this past weekend, Betty was thinking of suggesting to Jeremy that Kim could be sent back to Albany, but David's security team wanted her in the office and the condo so that action, would have to wait.

Kim was still hoping that Cameron would propose before her time to leave Miami. The attention and worry over Betty that weekend, was a nice change and the first time, that he had stayed overnight at her place. Kim had been so encouraged with his attentiveness and not wanting to go out, but instead, ordered in food and just watched movies while snuggling on the sofa or spending endless hours in bed. Until this weekend, Cameron had only taken her to hotels for the weekend and never during the weeknights. Kim had never gone to his place, and now wondered where he actually lived.

He was such an impeccable dresser and his cars were always detailed, she could not imagine his home would be any different. Last night, would have been a perfect opportunity to step up and take her to his home, so Betty could have Kim's room. After all the attention during the weekend, Kim thought they had really turned a corner in their relationship. Even with the wonderful romantic dinner on Sunday night, Cameron still dropped her off at the condo she shared with Betty, claiming he had to be at work early in the morning. She would have to talk very seriously with Cameron, as the project was wrapping up with a successful testing complete and the Go Live date scheduled for Thursday this week.

Jennifer phoned twice in the afternoon and Betty played it up when Kim was within earshot that 'no Jennifer you cannot go out clubbing and yes, we will have dinner in for the entire week until the doctor gives permission to fly.' Jennifer giggled in the background and Betty was aware she had moved into the bathroom with the change in sound. This was confirmed with the toilet flush and when the tap was running Jennifer was asking questions on the dark SUV. Naldo was still waiting on information for running the plates, but Arlo had picked it up near Betty's office, so he would be watching until Betty was safely home.

Betty stopped at the larger grocer on the way home and got all the groceries for her and Jennifer to finish within the week. Noting the volume of heavy bags having shopped for double her normal items, Betty felt justified on the cost of a taxi, for the 3 blocks home with a generous tip for the short distance. She pulled her phone out and was in the process of calling her preferred taxi firm when Kim came up to the till. Kim had been shopping for a few items herself, like it was a weekly occurrence. Betty did not point out to Kim, that the entire time in Miami, Kim had not even purchased a banana, but instead bit her tongue.

Kim squealed in delight to see Cameron waiting outside the grocer, in the same sedan as last evening. Of course, he would drive them home and even got out of the car to help Betty with her bags as Kim only had the two items, of milk and yogurt. Kim chatted all the way home, about what a long day it was at the office and Betty thought to herself as well, that it was, and now I have to watch for two additional containers in the fridge that will likely be spoilt.

At home, Jennifer pretended to be asleep, when Betty poked her head in her bedroom to check. Betty notably sighed in relief that she would be spared from an update on the current intrigue progress. She unpacked groceries and relaxed with the routine of chopping veggies for her chicken casserole recipe. Betty saw Cameron waiting on the sofa for Kim to freshen up from work. Hah! That is a lark, she did no work today, unless gabbing to co-workers was a project task that Betty missed in school.

"Cameron, would you and Kim care to stay for dinner?" Manners are manners and her mother would be appalled if the offer were not extended. After all, he did save her a taxi fare, and even carried in most of the bags.

Cameron turned to Betty's address like he had forgotten she was still there. "Augh… thanks, but no, I promised to take Kim to a new club."

Normally, manners would have dictated that Betty continue the conversation with a second offer, but frankly, she did not have the energy or the willingness to pursue and continued with the casserole preparation.

After the couple left, Betty checked on Jennifer again, and was surprised to find Jennifer still sleeping. Betty actually laid down on the sofa, willing herself to nap. There was still too much running around in her brain, and none of it was work. How did her life get so turned upside down by attending one work related party that she had not even wanted to attend? Had she simply stayed at home that night, none of this would be her problem. She would not be working with a security team to solve a corporate intrigue and attempted murder.

The owner of her contracted company would still be a mystery, not some tall, dark, handsome and well-built man. How is that for a cliché. And cliché or not he was truly that and much more as she vividly recalled every touch and kiss. It was less than three days and yet here she was, exhausted from a day of non-work and aching to be held in his arms.

She and Jennifer ate late and Betty ran the kitchen tap during clean-up to cover their talk of information gathered from the day. Kim came home after 11:00 p.m. and while Betty was asleep, Jennifer was still up, pretending to now be reading a fashion magazine, happy that Sally and Pirro missed nothing in their packing. Kim saw the light on and the door open, so checked, in on Jennifer as Jennifer hoped she would. Jennifer sighed. "Now I will have a slightly different breast size which will likely cause me to completely redo my entire wardrobe! Shopping for need is never as much fun. You get that, Betty sure doesn't."

Kim was in full agreement and they talked about dresses and shoes, and purses, and what club did Kim go to and who was there, and Kim spilled everything that Jennifer wanted, without even trying very hard.

Chapter 15

The second day of Jennifer's home convalescence began with Betty wanting an end, her body was stiff from sleeping on the sofa. Needing to listen to Kim for another day would be beyond torture. Luckily Kim was not up to help with breakfast and when Betty took a tray to Jennifer, Jennifer passed a note that in fact, it may end. Much information had been gathered and Josh was able to confirm the issue with the regulator, were all sourced from, Gainesville Enterprises. The SUV watching Betty yesterday also belonged to Gainesville Enterprises.

Betty was feeling there was finally an end in sight and it may not be the light of a train barrelling towards her. Josh still wanted Betty to watch Kim, but not to the extent as yesterday. They were completely convinced that Kim truly believed she was in a committed relationship with Cameron.

Betty gathered her lunch and workbag and knocked on Kim's door, as she would have in the past. Kim opened the door and asked Betty to wait for her, but Jennifer called from the other bedroom. "Betty don't forget my appointment with the doctor this afternoon, and of course I do need you to take me."

"I have not forgotten, and will order a taxi when I get to work." Betty rolled her eyes with the statement for Kim's view. "I need to run, as I have to leave early today. See you at the office." And with that Betty left the condo and set a fast pace for her walk to work, hoping it would help to stretch out the stiff muscles in her body.

The day for Betty was much like the first. Once settled at her desk, others in the office were full of new conversations. Apparently, Jeremy Marlin left at 12:00 p.m. yesterday with the owner and did not return. When Jeremy did arrive later than his usual time this morning, it was with the firm's lawyer. Apparently, the two went straight to Jeremy's office and the door remained closed since. Gossip and speculation by the staff was crazy and when asked by Kim or others, she was genuinely at a loss like everyone.

Betty worked through lunch and was surprised that no one else was in the building. If ever there was a time to stay at your desk and show dedication, it was surely a time when things appeared tenuous. Jeremy sent Betty a text before leaving with the lawyer for lunch, to update her, that all was fine and he would have more to tell her soon. So, it was a huge surprise to have Kim's boyfriend come by looking for Kim. Betty was really shocked and then almost got frightened that he was on to her and Jennifer, when the secretary returned to her desk and Kim's whereabouts was determined, causing Cameron to quickly leave to find her.

Kim finally returned to the office after a 2-hour lunch, and following a comment from the secretary, confirmed that no, she never did connect with Cameron. This sent Kim into an obvious state of panic that Betty noted as very uncharacteristic. Kim was generally so calm and assured of her relationship with Cameron that Betty felt it was worth reporting to the security team, how Kim was now busy texting Cameron.

Kim was deep in thought, after sending 2 text messages with no response, openly stating she had missed out on another opportunity with Cameron. She was asking others if it may be a sign that he stopped by her workplace at lunch. She should have never gone out and instead sat at her desk like boring Betty. Perhaps she would do this for the remainder of the week.

Betty left at 2:15 p.m. to walk home and on the way, ordered a taxi. As pre-arranged by Jennifer, the driver assigned was, Arlo. While walking, she was positive, she saw Cameron's car twice, but there were so many expensive cars, like his, around she could not be sure. If it were the flashy sporty one, it would be easier to identify, but the change to a sedan makes the identity less accurate.

Jennifer was acting extremely well, and Arlo as the driver was also in full form, pretending impatience and actually started the timer when they were coming out of the building. When they get into the car, Betty provided the address of the doctor's office and they drove off. Again, Betty was sure, she saw Cameron and once assured by Arlo, that the car was clean of bugs, Betty told Jennifer of her suspicions.

Arlo described a car and driver to the tee and this confirmed that Cameron was following Betty and Jennifer. Betty got nervous, but Jennifer and Arlo were happy. They wanted someone to be following them and the fact that it was Cameron himself was all the better.

The office building had a parking garage and rather than being released at the street curb and as pre-arranged, Arlo entered the parking garage with Cameron following. Betty and Jennifer stayed in form and exited the taxi, making a clear display of asking the driver to wait, including the payment of an extra 20 dollars. Arlo pocketed the bill and settled in to wait, by turning on his music and read a magazine.

Jennifer and Betty had no sooner entered the building when Cameron approached the taxi driver, and this was when 2 other men appeared and escorted Cameron into a private elevator, leaving Arlo to wait for his fare.

Within an hour, Betty and Jennifer come back to the cab and Arlo drove them home. The discussion in the car filled Betty in on a few things. This building was owned by David Baffa, outside of MDP. Cameron was the third son of, Samuel Lauther. The plan from the beginning of the project, was for Cameron to use Kim, unwittingly, to gather any information that could be used for a forced takeover of MDP.

Because MDP was fully by the book, the only remaining option had been to anonymously demand an audit by the regulator. With the MDP licenses being issued, noting David Baffa as owner, an audit would require David to be present at the audit, to defend his license. Having David incapacitated would cause the regulator to immediately suspend all licenses, allowing Gainesville Enterprises the much-needed opportunity for a hostile takeover.

Instead of going back to the condo, Arlo drove to Jeremy and Susan's residence for a dinner meeting. Betty left a message on Kim's cell phone, that she was taking Jennifer out for a quick dinner, after a great check-up with the doctor. Continued action plans for the software project wrap up and end to security concerns were completed as both friends and co-workers over Susan's salads and grillwork. Jeremy and Betty confirmed every business detail on their end and

Jennifer pouted that she would miss wearing the designer clothing and using expensive cosmetics. Arlo was confident this was only a joke, but made plans in his mind to speak to Sally and Pirro on every future occasion and eliminate stressful shopping trips for himself.

Later that night, Betty settled back on the sofa for her last uncomfortable sleep. It was hard to acknowledge David not having attended dinner that evening, and nor had he registered her presence in the office on Monday. Not even a covert phone call to check on her since leaving his home on Sunday. She resigned herself to another fitful sleep of berating herself for even remotely thinking that spending all weekend with a man and sharing kisses meant a relationship. It was time to go back to Albany, back to her parents and Julia, back to her own life. She had recovered from Peter; she would recover from David as well.

Chapter 16

Betty rose on Wednesday with a sense of dread and at the same time anticipation. The plan outlined last evening as a group was solid, functional and would put an end to this circus her life had become. She was surprised to have slept at all with her spinning thoughts. Her resolution to put any continued romance with Mr David Baffa out of the realm of reality, but instead held it as a blessed memory and had allowed her mind to compartmentalise the weekend experience of physical contact and expression, to remain firm in her mind that she was capable of having a wonderful physical relationship. No, that was not true, she deserved to have only a loving physical relationship.

This self-awareness had been processed in her mind during her sleep, so that she would accept nothing less. Peter had not loved her in a way she deserved, that was a fact. If David was just playing games and using her as a means to an end, then she would learn from that experience as well. She did not need to be settling any longer. Betty had watched the relationship of her own parents and while not perfect, it was truly whole. They made mistakes as do any couple, but what sustained their relationship and marriage was the willingness to be respectful, loving and kind to each other. Why was this awareness such a revelation to her? Why, after growing up, in such an inclusive environment of love, had she ever accepted Peter's lack of commitment to her? He obviously did not lack commitment, as displayed by his marriage, not soon after leaving her. Peter not being committed to her was unacceptable and for this she had only herself to blame, for having spent too many years in a situation that was unfulfilling and unrewarding. Well, that had ended with a huge summary of lessons learned. She had her career, and a great one at that! She loved her work, her family, Julia and other friends, that she was blessed to have in her life. Being alone would be a choice, not a life sentence of loneliness. She did not need a man to make her whole. Betty McDowall, was whole on her own and if a man wanted to join her, it would be as his own person and a compliment to her, with love and commitment.

This resolve carried Betty into the shower and preparation for work. Jennifer found Betty in the kitchen making coffee and breakfast humming. "Good morning, coffee and eggs?"

Jennifer found the smell of coffee revolting, and the mention of eggs caused a violent reaction to her already weak stomach. "Neither thanks! I will just boil the water for some of that peppermint tea. Surprising how much I really like it. Who knew?"

Betty had been feeding the tea to Jennifer since her return on Sunday, perhaps it had helped Jennifer change from her 10 plus cups of coffee, to something more healthy. "Sure, but no eggs or toast?"

"Toast yes, but no butter. I have disabled the recording bug so we can talk freely. But, I think I have been playing the sick routine too well as I feel like I have a bug this morning."

Jennifer had woken fine, but the smell from the kitchen had turned it around rapidly, after opening the bedroom door.

"You are likely missing Sally's kitchen. I like to cook, but my skills are basic compared to Sally's expertise. What Sally prepares is inspired creativity that is delivered onto the plate with passionate devotion!" Betty was confident in her kitchen abilities but having tasted Sally's creations, knew she was nowhere near Sally's level of cooking and baking.

Jennifer smiled at the compliment and whispered. "I will be sure to tell Sally that." Both the ladies heard movement from Kim's room and switched to the plan, as Jennifer continued in a normal speaking voice. "I should hear from the doctor's office by mid-morning, and hopefully it will give me the clearance to fly home tonight. I would love to take you to a nice dinner after work, to thank you for all your kindness. Plus, this whole experience was wrong to hide from my parents, so I will be going straight home to them when I land and confess everything." Jennifer was following the script completely.

"Dinner sounds lovely, even though it is not necessary. Greatly appreciated, but not necessary." Betty needed to stay true to herself and not tip Kim off in anyway. "Let's just wait to hear that you are cleared to fly, and if it takes another day of healing, then we will postpone our dinner one day."

"Fair enough, but my stiches and strips are itchy, which is a true sign of healing according to the doctor. I can have them removed on Friday back home and they made that appointment before I left the office yesterday. Now that I am resolved to come clean to Mum and Dad, I want to get home, get it done and move forward." Jennifer was beginning to have colour in her cheeks with the tea and plain toast, plus her stomach was settling with the food.

Kim had entered the common area during the latter part of the conversation. "Jennifer it will be sad to see you leave, I was hoping to chat more on your choice of shops. Could I get your email and number so we can stay in contact? I would love to come out to California for a vacation. Plus, after this successful project who knows where the next opportunity will be."

Jennifer had her back to Kim, sitting at the kitchen nook and raised her eyebrows to Betty before turning around and answering. "You would love California, Kim! I will write out my digits and we can text all the time."

Betty wanted to be sick with Jennifer's comment, but had to admit it was something her cousin would say. "Oh Kim, before I forget, I had text message from Jamel. Apparently, she has to take her grandmother to a medical appointment today so will not be in until tomorrow."

Kim, at first had no care of the cleaning day, until she realised the impact to herself. "Well, that won't work, I have dry cleaning being delivered and picked up today. I am not sure I can reschedule that; I have to find their card and call them." Kim turned to go back into her room to search for the contact information.

Jennifer quickly solved Kim's issues. "I will be here all day, and not napping anymore. I will be here for the regular delivery." Then turning to Betty. "Plus, I can have them take that wonderful dress you were wearing Friday, when you came to be with me and give them very clear instructions to resurrect from the plastic bag you tossed it into. If I leave today, the cleaner will come after I have gone so, I am not disturbed by her fussing." Jennifer was becoming a pro at being just a taste of nasty.

"Jennifer, I so appreciate that; they have my card information on file so no need to worry about payment and I will leave my bag in the entry, just hang the returned there. I will sort it out when I get home." Kim was relieved to have her problem solved.

Betty thought that Kim was completely absorbed in such first-world problems like dry cleaning. No thought of people that did not have proper clothing, much less clean clothing. Well, after today Kim would not be her problem anymore. "I will also set out my dress. I think I tossed it in the bottom of my closet to deal with later." Betty headed into her room to deal with the task.

This time it was for Kim's benefit that Jennifer rolled her eyes and whispered. "I am not sure she will ever appreciate fashion. No wonder she has no man." Kim giggled at Jennifer's comment and nodded in agreement.

In Kim's mind, Betty was not unattractive. Given the correct cosmetics, hairstyle and products, great clothes, essentially a full makeover, she would do well at the clubs and have lots of dates like, Cameron. Well not Cameron, as he was hers. Just someone like Cameron. She would talk to Betty after Jennifer left; it was the perfect opportunity to bring up the subject again. Lord knew, she had tried a few times after arriving in Miami, but this would be one last effort that could have great results. She would even talk to Cameron, to see if he had a suitable friend, that would not take advantage of Betty's lack of experience. This could be a wonderful turning point for Betty!

Jennifer began her own packing after the ladies left for work and opened the door to Sally, Pirro and Arlo within the hour, who were armed with boxes and packing material. After a quick greeting, Sally and Pirro attacked Kim's room. Arlo gathered Jennifer in his arms and was shocked to see, that regardless of the extensive resting and relaxing for a few days she appeared more tired than when leaving the house on Sunday. "I love you my dear, but you are seeing a doctor today." Arlo squeezed Jennifer tighter to quash her protests and then released her to reiterate his point. "No arguments. I have made an appointment and as soon as we are packed up, I will be taking you myself." Smiling to assure Jennifer that he will not be leaving her side.

"No argument, today I actually felt ill, as well as tired. If I have a bug, it needs to leave, so that I am in top form for my job as well as for you, my love. Plus, this is the first time since we have been together that I have not slept in your arms. So, if your arms are around me all day and tonight, I am sure I will feel better." Jennifer held Arlo's forehead to her own conveying every emotion of gratitude, to having found such a dedicated love and life partner.

Sally popped out from Kim's bedroom. "Ok, I get the reunion, but let's get this done. I have lunch to make and looks like you need a fresh batch of cinnamon buns."

Jennifer laughed at the thought of cinnamon buns and was surprised to find her mouth-watering in anticipating. "Right you are! Arlo my bags are ready in Betty's room. Betty also confirmed that there is nothing of Kim's outside of her bedroom, except for the bag for the drycleaner that we can pack as is. There will be a delivery shortly according to Jamel's confirmation of their schedule. Let's get Kim out of

Betty's life." With that, the team had the entire contents of Kim's room boxed and labelled for shipment including the final drycleaner delivery within an hour.

Pirro had been the one to write out specific instructions to accompany about Betty's dress and to confirm the closure of Kim's account. Sally made them coffee at the condo and set out a plate of her own morning batch of banana bread, while they waited for the pick up by the shipping company. Kim had been wise to hold her rented room in the shared house back in Albany and a roommate had agreed to be present to receive the delivery for a price, of course.

Betty had survived the incessant chatter and plan for her makeover by Kim during their walk to the office, by nodding in agreement and providing one-word answers. The short walk in the morning sunlight was generally a source of enjoyment for Betty. Soaking up the morning sunlight while being in full gratitude to God and the universe for having this wonderful opportunity, was part of her routine to greet a new workday. There was no gratitude for Kim's chatter and the morning blessing was spoiled and tainted by Kim's verbal diarrhoea and negative critique of Betty's entire appearance.

Betty's mood did not improve once reaching the office. Jeremy's office door was closed and clearly, he was not alone in there. This situation had caused the office buzz of gossip and speculation to run ramped. Betty felt so drained by the time her coffee mug was prepared, that she plated a sugary and sprinkled donut to take to her desk as a source of indulgence and false fortification for the day ahead. She muttered a conference call to the secretary and proceeded with the rare closing of her office door, to give herself some peace.

Betty completed the motions of donning her telephone headset and completing a call with the general mouthing of verbiage for a phone call. She even focused her eyes on the false documents opened on her computer screen with the apt appearance of diligent note taking to show full commitment. But the attempt at serenity did not last for more than a few minutes. Even with the closed door, the outburst invaded her quiet space, as Kim made her way to her desk and attempted a login. "Is anyone else having issues? Where is James to get my passwords reset? This has never happened before? Is anyone else having this problem?" Kim was accustomed to everyone jumping to her rescue, that it was actually a shock to be receiving no immediate support. James, the office technical support expert, was uncharacteristically absent. No one else was experiencing issues with access to the network. With a huff, Kim sat at her desk after being told that James would not be in the office until the afternoon. "There must be someone else that can fix this?" The secretary returned a gesture of no.

The general office noise level picked up again, as Rodger, the junior manager, rose from his desk with an email from Mr Baffa, asking him to invite everyone in the office to join him in a breakfast celebration, being catered for them in the empty office space next door. Smiles and chatter erupted at the exciting treat announcement and all staff rose to follow the junior manager, as if he were the Pied Piper.

Kim went to Betty's office window to signal the mass exodus and Betty used hand signals to reiterate her call continuing longer and a wave to indicate that Kim should go with the crowd. Kim shrugged her shoulders and happily turned to skip along with the others.

Jeremy's office door opened at that moment and asked Kim to come and join him. This was not unusual, as Jeremy often asked staff in, to discuss a task assignment or issue. But what weakened Kim's knees, causing her to drop into the remaining vacant chair of Jeremy's office, was the presence of a man, Kim knew to be the company legal counsel and Jeremy closing his office door.

With Kim in Jeremy's office and the remaining staff absent, Betty pulled a prepared box from under her own desk that Jeremy had said he would leave. In the quiet of the main-office, it was actually sad to be packing up the desk of a co-worker. Betty could not help but think, what it would be like to have someone do this for her. Not a pleasant thought at all, so Betty took care to ensure items were wrapped to avoid breakage. Files did not need to be packed as they belonged to MDP and Betty would sort those back at her own desk. Surprisingly, everything fit into the one box and Betty was just affixing the shipping label, when the arranged pick up arrived. This box would be shipped with the condo items and delivered to Kim's rental in Albany, by the end of the business day.

Betty put Kim's files on her own desk and followed the deliveryman out of the office to join the breakfast party next door. Bart Hartley, her boss at Flow-Soft in Albany, had indicated that Betty should not be present when Kim left the office. Bart was still unsure of what would await Kim on her return, and more than likely, it would be dependent on Kim's reaction and attitude for wanting to continue her employment upon her return.

Kim exited Jeremy's office in a brain fog. Nothing had ended as she wanted or had hoped. Learning that Cameron was using her for information only was a major blow, but now, even her employment was in question. It was a huge relief for Kim to find the office empty when she stepped into the common office area, but then she remembered they were all celebrating next door without her.

Bill Rhodes, legal counsel for MDP, had his hand lightly on Kim's elbow to steer her out of the office, into the waiting town car. Betty had left Kim's purse on her desk and Jeremy scooped this up, as he followed Bill, leading Kim from the office.

Bill was gentle with his assistance of placing Kim in the backseat of the waiting car. If the situation was not so entirely surreal, Kim would have thought the man was treating her as if on a date. Bill settled beside Kim, to accompany her to the airport and accepted the purse from Jeremy before closing the door with a signal for the driver to proceed.

Jeremy turned back towards the office to see Betty standing at the window of the adjacent office watching Kim leave. He had no appetite for food or a wish to address his staff. He just needed a few minutes to compose his thoughts. It was not his first time escorting an employee from the premises, but in the past, the individual being terminated was fully aware of either, their incompetence or unethical actions. Kim had truly been the definition of a patsy. She was guilty of taking advantage of the role with MDP, and her work was only at par in Jeremy's mind, but she did not deserve to be so obviously devastated to learn of Cameron's duplicity.

Betty watched Kim leave and had seen only a glimpse of her devastation. Betty prayed she would hear Jeremy confirm that Cameron had used her and there was no knowledge of the poisoning on Kim's part. She also knew what a soft heart

Jeremy had and was not surprised to see him look defeated as well, when he turned back to the office. Betty waved to acknowledge seeing each other and was prepared to leave him to his thoughts. Instead, Jeremy returned the wave with an added gesture for her to come back to the main office with him.

Jeremy had a planned a speech for the staff regarding Kim's absence. They were planning to tell everyone that Kim's mother was ill and she had been urgently called home by her family. With the project wrapping up, MDP was happy to assist with her family emergency and had made all of her travel and shipping arrangements. It would be up to Kim whether a different story ever came to light.

Betty walked back into Jeremy's office and found him wiping his eyes. "Are you ok? Was Kim a pill?"

"Sorry, no she was not. All I can think of right now is this happing to one of my own daughters or even you. She was truly shocked when Bill laid out all the information and was most cooperative with her own information. Cameron really played her, Betty. She truly believed that Cameron would propose marriage before Flow-Soft called her back to Albany. That is just heart breaking and mean on his part. I hope the judge puts this Cameron boy in jail for a few years, to think about using other people for his father's gain." Jeremy was moving from sad to angry, thinking of Cameron's part.

Betty patted his hand. "Your girls are far too smart for someone like Cameron, and I would like to think that I am as well. Kim was lucky to have you with her, that Mr Rhodes scares me just with his lawyer look. Did he go into courtroom mode?"

"No courtroom antics were needed, and actually he was very kind to Kim. He was clear and precise with all the legal facts, but soon realised Kim held no fault. He is even staying with her until she gets on the plane, to ensure she is cared for. I know that he can be intimidating, but it was nice to see such a kind side today." Jeremy truly smiled at his recollection of Bill being so gentle putting Kim in the car.

"Well, it is nice to know that sharks have a soft side. I hope the flight gives Kim some time to think, before Bart picks her up in Albany. I am not sure she will ever get such a good position as she has with Flow-Soft, and with some positive coaching I would work with her again. Just not be roommates." Betty and Jeremy were able to share a quiet laugh before they heard the noise of staff returning from breakfast.

They waited until everyone was back at their desks, and then together left his office to update the staff on Kim's immediate exit. Offers to text or send emails of compassion were quickly discussed, and Betty ended this chatter by saying that Kim just needed a day or two of alone time with her family and then she would likely provide an update to all her friends.

Chapter 17

The remainder of Wednesday was rather anti-climactic for Betty. The office was calm and quiet without Kim stirring up gossip. Betty noted this in her summary to Bart as something that would be beneficial to discuss with Kim, on a personal improvement level at her next review, should she choose to stay with Flow-Soft.

The application Go-live for the new software was proceeding as scheduled for tonight, so she would be on call if there were any issue. As this was a new installation, there was no risk of existing data in the current environment. It would be the Thursday morning testing by the staff, to ensure that, all the data was transferred over in a correct fashion. These tests were already planned for the next morning and Jeremy was planning to have all staff available for the testing, including the need to stretch it to the evening if necessary. With such a busy day and the possible need for Friday morning, Jeremy had planned a surprise lunch for the staff on Friday, at a local sports bar with an afternoon of playtime at the facility. Both lunch and fun, was booked for both, staff and contractors as a thanks.

Betty was so grateful to be in a second organisation that not only valued their staff, but also saw the added value of rewarding them, on a continuous basis. She was not sure if this was Jeremy and her own boss, Bart comparing management styles, and was being supported by David Baffa, as the owner, or if this was also David's management style?

How could she ever know the answer to this thought, as the man was an absent owner and had been unknown to herself and many of his own staff until the party at his home, last Friday. Good grief, was that only last Friday? This week had been such a whirlwind of emotion and intrigue, that Betty felt like caring for David and being in his arms for almost 24 hours, had happened months ago.

There was still no direct contact from David, and Betty was pleased with herself for seeing this as just a single incident to be cherished, for only a small slice of time that had greatly shown her some insight to her own worth. Kim's talk about a makeover was not completely wrong for her, only the extreme methods and changes outlined were not a fit for Betty. That being said, she would talk with Julia this evening, to make a plan for either in Florida when Julia's schedule allowed for a visit, or waiting until back in Albany, some changes were in her future.

Betty thought of, new make-up, a fresh haircut, perhaps some highlights, that would grow out nicely. Then thinking of the beautiful green silk dress from Friday night, perhaps a splurge on some lavish new pieces, to perk up her wardrobe, were also in order. She would text Julia now and set the stage for a great chat tonight, with her dear friend.

Betty returned to the condo that evening to find that Jamel had thoroughly cleaned and changed linens in her own room, but Kim's was complete as well. She started a draft for her note of thanks, with a reminder for an extra tip to Jamel next week. Betty also wondered if, Pirro and Sally had stayed to assist, but she could send them thanks later as well. She sat at the dining table looking out at the orange and pinks of the sunset, enjoying a light salad for dinner. The stillness of having this space to herself had come at Kim's expense, and a price much higher than she had paid with Peter. She said a prayer, that Kim would accept Bart's offer to stay and rebuild her career, and that she could also assist in that restart for Kim.

As the dark shade of evening lowered, Betty cleared away dishes and replaced them with her phone, laptop and ear buds to start a great conversation with Julia, to look at different websites for style ideas. Julia confirmed, that she was due some extra time, and preferred the option of coming to Miami for a fun vacation, rather than waiting for Betty to return home.

Betty's voice had a spark, that Julia had been waiting for almost a year, to see return to her cherished friend and was more than willing to be the director of such an exciting production. Betty fired off a text to Susan Marlin for suggestions as well, knowing if there was a valued resource, why do the leg work on your own. And in all the excitement of planning, Betty totally missed the two times that Julia hinted at having something of her own to share.

Betty received a text just after 10:00 p.m. from James, technical support of MDP, saying the installation and data transfer had been completed with no error messages or issues. All was ready for the testing by the staff the next morning. He was headed home, but would be back in the office as usual, with the staff to be present for anything that could possibly show. No longer a need for being on call herself, Betty headed off to bed, her own bed with fresh bedding. She drifted off to sleep thinking of all the website images for a new look.

The Thursday morning walk to work was again a walk of gratitude and anticipation, of not only a successful completion to her project, but the anticipation of Julia's visit and all the fun they would have shopping and checking out salons.

The staff gathered for a quick stand-up meeting as Betty had planned. There was coffee and treats for the staff to keep them fortified and a light lunch would be brought in so that everyone could just focus on testing without too much of an interruption to their regular tasks. A new system was always a tough change, and regardless of involvement, testing, engagement and buy-in, it always had components of resistance. Betty was happy to be staying for at least another month, to be present to add individual training and coaching.

She had clearly laid out process changes that flowed smoothly on a chart, but did not always flow well with data input and reporting. Betty made it clear to each staff member, ensuring to engage with individual eye contact, she was there to help everyone transition smoothly and with full knowledge. These were valued and dedicated MDP staff members, and anything she could do to add to their experience, was in Betty's mind, worth every minute of her time.

The day proceeded with generally expected issues and concerns, that always came with testing a new system once the data was live. Often, it was just a reminder to follow the desk manuals that had been prepared for each staff position. Reminding someone to get up and take a break with a short walk or stretch while waiting for incoming data to finish processing.

Reports were running a little slower than expected, so James asked everyone to log out of the system and enjoy a lunch break, while he applied a small patch to the database. By late afternoon, everyone had finished testing and was happy with the results. Jeremy was thrilled to announce an early end to the day for all with a personal handshake to each staff member, for their focused work that day. Another nice personal touch in Betty's mind.

Betty was in the process of tidying her desk for the day as well, when Bill Rhodes entered her office. Betty tried to hold her surprise internally and covered by asking if Jeremy should be present as well. Bill completely agreed and they quietly moved to the other office. As the three settled in Jeremy's office, Bill outlined his efforts in court for the past few days. "Well, I am happy to report, that all seems to be wrapping up rather well with your assistance Betty."

"Cameron has taken a lesser plea and given up his father and oldest brother which will be settled as a separate matter with the courts and the regulator. Cameron will only do 6 months for poisoning Mr Baffa and then probation for 5 years, but his record will not have an attempted-murder charge, as I originally demanded. Thanks to your formal statement we had enough for the District Attorney to make that case, but as his father is a much bigger fish for the DA, the plea bargain was a justified sacrifice."

"Well, that is a huge relief! Don't you agree Betty?" Jeremy was happy there would not be a court case.

"I do agree, but sad that Kim was a bit of a victim in this scheme. Will there be any implication for her?" Betty truly felt sorry for Kim. She had let herself be a victim, but after her own experience with Peter, she was well aware that it was hard to see the truth, when you are in the thick of a situation.

"Kim is completely in the clear, and as another note, I heard from your Mr Hartley, that when he and the human resource advisor met Kim's plane, she was fully prepared to cooperate and learn from her experience. Mostly meaning that she would be focusing on her work, rather than socialising for the time being. She is a very lovely young lady, and I doubt she will go long without a few dates." Bill smiled as he thought of Kim. She was so sad when he put her on the plane, north, were he 20 years younger and not married, he would have asked for her number himself.

"That is nice to hear. People make mistakes all the time, including me. It is how we recover and move forward from those mistakes that truly define us. I was telling Jeremy that I would work with Kim again, just not wanting to share accommodation again." Betty was smiling as Jeremy returned her smile.

"Betty you are far too generous. Kim is lucky to have you in her corner." Then turning his attention back to Bill, Jeremy asked what remained unanswered. "So that takes care of Cameron, but what will happen with Sam Lauther and his son? Will that be a new court case that will involve Betty?"

Bill looked directly at Betty. "It will be a separate case. I am not sure how the DA will proceed, and it will go before the grand jury early next week. If it does go to trial, you may be called to testify." Bill saw the shock on Betty's face and was quick to reassure. "Don't worry, this will be very simple and Mr Baffa has asked me to represent and coach you, should this be required. You will be a very minor part of their case and testimony."

"Well, that is certainly generous of Mr Baffa, and Bill, I do appreciate your support, but I can hire my own lawyer, should it become necessary. I would not want to put you in any position of conflict of interest or whatever it is, they call a lawyer representing the same parties." Betty was rather miffed that David had talked of her to Bill, but not talked to her at all. Well, that was just another sign of where their relationship, or lack thereof stood!

"Not a conflict at all, and I am MDP counsel so you are covered under that umbrella as a contractor. I will keep you informed. Jeremy tells me that you are her for another month, so hopefully everything will be wrapped up by then." Bill thought it strange, that Betty did not understand David wanting to protect her. His conversations with David this past week had always included her protection. Very strange indeed, that she was not aware of this.

Bill left the office and Jeremy mentioned meeting Susan for a casual dinner. Betty was invited to join them, and with an empty condo to return to, it was a much-preferred option to avoid a boring salad. Dinner with the Marlin's was just like being with her own parents, so she and Jeremy wrapped up quickly to meet Susan.

Chatter at dinner included a review of Susan's lists of shops and salons for Julia's upcoming visit and Betty's impending makeover. There was discussion of relief that David was healthy and the Lauther family was not a threat to Betty.

It was over the indulgence of a chocolate layer cake for dessert, that Jeremy and Susan shared a quick look of agreement and then Jeremy addressed Betty. "There is another reason we wanted to have dinner with you. Susan's accident last week shook some things up for us and we wanted to talk to you out of the office."

"Oh, my lord! Susan are you all right? Did you get hurt from that accident and have it not shown-up until the next day?" Betty was panicked and babbled. It would be a similar blow, as having one of her parents' health be at risk.

Susan held up her hand for Betty to stop talking. "Relax, I am fine. No current health issues, no effects from the accident. But the accident itself made us take a hard look at our life and our age."

Betty was looking intently back and forth between Susan and Jeremy, still questioning what this meant. "So, your fine." Addressing Susan with relief. "Is it you that is sick Jeremy?" Betty turned her attention to him.

"No! No one is sick, we are both very happy and healthy." Jeremy replied, rather exasperated. This was not being handled well at all. Clear things up quick he thought. "What the accident made us decide is, that we want to enjoy our age, and that means me not working as hard as I do, possibly even part time, and eventually completely retiring. We want to travel and enjoy our family. My entire career was built to provide for my family."

"Susan would fill me in and keep me informed, but I was not there every day for the little experiences. I want to be present at home more, and less at the office." Jeremy had turned to take Susan's hand and stare at her lovely face. In his eyes, she still looked the same as when they married and Jeremy wanted more moments looking into those eyes.

Betty choked-up at the expression of love. It was wonderful to see couples be tender and in love at this age. She could hardly fault Jeremy for wanting to take a step towards

173

retirement. He had worked hard and more than paid his dues, now it was time to bask in the rewards and spend time with Susan.

"I never once faulted a minute you spent at the office, building your career. It provided a wonderful life for our family and when you were home, you were always home 110%, with both love and interest in our family. But having you home more would truly be a blessing." Susan still felt she was the luckiest woman in the world, having Jeremy as her husband, partner, and lover. The two kissed with tears in their eyes and broke apart with a laugh of shared tenderness. "Sorry, we should not be making a spectacle in public."

Betty brushed away the tears from her own cheeks and smiled. "Of course, you should, after so many years it is rather nice to know, that this level of love and happiness is actually attainable. My own parents are equally as fortunate. However, would never be caught kissing in public, but that is them and I know even without the public display, it is there."

Jeremy blushed lightly at Susan and then returned his focus to Betty. "What we really wanted to ask you, and I have Mr Baffa's approval to do so, is to offer you the assistant manager's position at MDP. Rodger, the current junior manager as accepted a role with Baffa Holdings, the real estate company that David owns. That has left a vacancy that would not be easy to fill, and one that I would be able to quickly train you, in both the business and system knowledge. You have both, with your software knowledge and the business knowledge from implementing software. You are the preferred candidate. Please say yes, Betty." Jeremy reached across the table to take her hand, as he could see that brilliant mind whirling at a hundred miles per hour.

Betty looked down at his hand to confirm that it was real. Then looked back at both Susan and Jeremy attempting to find her voice and rational speech to flow from her mouth. "Wow! I was not expecting that. Wow! I am shocked, honoured that you think that much of my work, but shocked. I can't imagine staying in Miami, and not returning to my parents and friends. What will Julia say if I stay here permanently? What will Bart think of me if I take this offer?" Betty knew she was babbling, but questions and scenarios were churning in her mind at such a rapid rate, that she was rather overwhelmed.

Jeremy could see she was overwhelmed and wanted to provide a calming effect to her decision. He squeezed her hand to confirm he was still with her. "I see this is more of a shock than, I thought it would be. I am actually surprised you did not see this coming. Many of the staff come to you before they come to me, and often it is you bringing them to me with a solution in mind that just needs my approval to implement. You have their trust and respect and that is of utmost importance for a good manager. David and I both spoke to Bart, he is well aware that we will be making this offer, it is not behind his back. He said that he would be devastated to lose you, but only wanted the best for your career."

"You and David talked to Bart behind my back?" Betty was stunned and insulted. "I am not surprised that you would talk to Bart, he is your friend, but David? Mr Baffa, who I did not even meet until Friday night and has never been in the office to see my work, but has the gall to discuss me with my employer behind my back!" Betty was not just insulted, now she was mad. How dare the man!

"Hold on!" Jeremy was not expecting this reaction as all. "Hold on and let's just settle down please." Jeremy was begging Betty to relax.

But it was Susan with the calming voice. "Betty, Jeremy is not the enemy here and I am sorry you are hurt with discussions happening without your knowledge. In hindsight, I think that I would be equally upset. Can we please just talk about this calmly?"

Betty inhaled a very deep and calming breath. She closed her eyes to feel the air fill her lungs and then slowly released it, as instructed by her therapist. When she opened her eyes, both Susan and Jeremy were staring in anticipation of another eruption. "I am sorry Jeremy, that was not called for and very unprofessional of me. It has been a very long week and the drama involving David has been a lot. I am sorry."

Jeremy nodded his acceptance of her apology but it was Susan that continued. "Jeremy has been keeping me up to date with the attempt on Mr Baffa, and how you saved him. That must have been very scary. Plus, on top of that sending Kim home and the system going live, that is more than enough drama for a year, much less a week. Perhaps we should call it an evening and get you home so you can think about the offer through with space and quiet and let you and Jeremy talk tomorrow."

"I appreciate that, Susan. I really do, but I am not sure if I can accept the offer. There was a lot that went on caring for Mr Baffa that you do not know and I am not sure that I can stay here and work for him." Betty was very articulate and precise in her words wanting to be very clear that her decision to accept the offer would likely be a no.

"Jeremy, why don't you go for a walk around the block and let Betty and I have a chat?" This was not a question but an order for Jeremy to follow without question.

He looked at his wife and then over at Betty, who still appeared to be in a state of shock. But he had received a similar suggestion, when Susan wanted to pry something from one or both of their daughters, so he rose from the table. "Perhaps you are correct my dear, I think a walk is in order. I will be back shortly." And with that Jeremy made his exit.

Susan smiled at his quick pick up and promised herself that a huge reward, later in bed, was well deserved. Then she gave herself a little shake for courage and turned her attention back to Betty. "Betty look at me." It was the direct order of a parent to child. Which Betty responded to, by raising her eyes to be level with Susan's. "Obviously, there was much more went on last weekend between you and David Baffa. How about you get it out and let's get through it."

"My mother does that. How did you know that?" Betty found it a little creepy that Susan could almost read her mind.

"What can I say, it is a mother thing. Wait till you have your own children, you will have it as well." Susan smiled at the mother acknowledgement, she hated it when her own mother had done this, but found it very beneficial as a mother of two girls. "Anyway, still waiting… spill!" It was a command, not request now.

Betty laughed and shook her head. She had no idea what or how to tell someone, so she just started at the beginning, or rather the end of her conversation with Susan and Jeremy Friday evening at David's house. She relayed everything in detail, from the scare of caring for the man, to the intimate contact, to the wonder of the stairwell light, to the kiss before leaving his home on Sunday. She finally ended with not having had any contact with the man all week. No call, no text, no email. Nothing!

Betty was rather drained at the end, and then relief poured in, at finally telling someone what had happened. She had not even told Julia everything, as she had promised not to say a word, to hide the story of Jennifer in her home. "I have never been so confused in my life. Can you now see why I have no interest or desire to stay in Miami and be an employee of this jerk, who can talk to others about me, but not to me!"

Susan was rather stunned herself with the story. She had met Mr Baffa on Friday night very briefly and thought of him as very tall, dark and handsome, but he had been rather rude at the time, and now Susan realised he must have been starting to feel very ill at their meeting. "I knew you stayed with him all weekend, but had no idea he kissed you! And not just as a show to his staff and being watched, but he kissed you very privately before you left on Sunday. No wonder you are so confused. What game is he playing?" Susan was beginning to feel anger as well towards this Mr Baffa.

"I owe Jeremy the truth as well, to go with my apology. This is a mess for me personally and a great opportunity, but considering everything, I am not sure I can accept a position with MDP. Do you understand that, Susan?" Betty was feeling much calmer for having told Susan everything, but still felt accepting Jeremy's offer was not a good move for her personally.

"I do understand, but want to ask you to take the evening and even the weekend before you formally decline the offer. You may not change your mind with your decision, but at least you will be able to say that you took the necessary time to properly consider your decision." Susan wanted Betty to stay in Miami for very selfish reasons. She had become very special to her and Jeremy, almost like another daughter. Plus, with Betty, the transition to Jeremy's retirement would be seamless. But having heard the intimate contact with Mr Baffa, she also understood that Betty needed to protect her heart.

"I am not sure my decision will change, but I do promise to give the offer some time and a logical review. Will you tell Jeremy my whole weekend story?" Betty was lucky to have someone like Susan in Miami. It helped to lessen the absence of her mother.

"I promise to leave that to you if you chose. However, if the answer is no, please tell him everything, so that he fully understands your decision." Susan received a nod of acceptance from Betty. "I know Jeremy paid the tab before going out, so let's find him and get you home. I am available for a chat anytime and promise not to bring my selfish agenda into your decision process, if asked for assistance." Susan was happy to have Betty calm and back on track. She was a smart young lady with the confidence to make the right decision.

"I would appreciate you trying not to tell him all the details. If he presses you and something slips, do not feel too guilty, just send me a text to let me know. I want to think over the weekend as you suggested and I will tell him all the details myself with my answer on Monday. I am so grateful to have you here Susan, I hope I tell you often how much I cherish our friendship." Betty was sincere and wanted to ensure Susan knew this to be the truth.

The ladies had exited the restaurant to find Jeremy waiting by the parked car. "I cherish our friendship as well. I think I can hold him off until Monday." Susan smiled at Jeremy and as he had seen this look many times over the years, was happy to accept Betty's thanks for dinner and the ride home.

Chapter 18

Betty spent a horribly restless night. She osculated between accepting Jeremy's offer and rejecting it. How could she work under the employ of a man who had so jangled and disrupted her emotions and then dropped her like a dirty t-shirt.

The idea of a dirty t-shirt only served as a very bad metaphor. Because then her mind flipped back to Friday night and the discarding of her clothing all over his bedroom, mimicking the throws of passion. How she had wished for that passion to be real!

Wearing his t-shirt for sleep had barely covered her and lying next to him, feeling his arms holding her had been like a dream come true. The kiss in the morning for the camera had been so much more than acting on her own part, as were the other intimate moments shared during the remainder of the weekend.

Betty realised around 2:00 a.m. that she had fallen in love with Mr David Baffa in less than 24 hours! The realisation was the greatest cause of her pain, plus knowing that the love was not returned. The acknowledgement of love, was in a way comforting, as well as painful. It was comforting to know that she was capable of such deep feelings for another man. In retrospect, her relationship with Peter over the years had never reached the level of deep emotional attachment as she had with David in such a short time. The comfort of this honesty to herself was then almost like a physical pain of a knife, cutting into her heart with the reminder of his absence from her life since leaving his home on Sunday.

She was not young anymore, but the illusion of his silence and absence was clearly understood with her limited relationship maturity. She had just watched Kim give everything of herself to Cameron for the past months and had paid a much higher price than Betty ever had with Peter. Kim would be hurt and devastated, but in the process of giving to Cameron had almost lost her career as well.

Betty was not willing to sacrifice her career for any man, and was thankful that her work, along with family and Julia, had pulled her through Peter walking out of her life. If she took the position with MDP, it would require a very clear contract outlining her management autonomy in the office and insist on limited contact with David. The form of negotiation was necessary in her mind to avoid another episode of the past weekend. Good grief, just the past weekend, and her life had turned a complete 180 degrees from the calm structure she had worked so hard to attain, following Peter.

If she returned to Albany and continued with Flow-Soft her plans would continue as previously outlined. She would find a place of her own. Furnish it to suit only herself. She would even buy a car that she wanted. Her career would continue to fill her days. Julia and she would spend such wonderful evenings and weekends going to shows and shopping. It would all be back to normal and safe in Albany... and horribly boring and lonely!

Shit, shit, shit! She wanted the excitement of David. This past week had been the most excitement she had ever had in her life. Plus, she wanted him! Staying in Miami and in his employ would keep him in her sights. She could revise that contract to insist on weekly, no bi-weekly meetings that would force her into his purview. She could use that time to remind him of their weekend together and how she had saved his life. Kim would do that and so could she.

Well, she could try to do that. Maybe. Maybe not. That was not her style. She could not even imagine trying something so underhanded. Better to run back to Albany and be lonely forever. That she was sure of. Loneliness would be her new norm, because the thought of another man ever filling her heart the way David had, in less than 24 hours seemed about as likely as Betty moving to Mars.

Betty must have drifted off to sleep eventually, as she woke to her alarm blaring and her head feeling like she had consumed an entire bottle of red wine with dinner, rather than the one glass, nursed during the entire time at the restaurant. Her walk to work was still one of gratitude, as she was thankful for the opportunity of staying in Miami, but her decision to return home to Albany was truly the only option available for her sanity.

The morning at the office flowed calmly and efficiently, with no issues using the new software program. The office staff moved to the sports bar for lunch and an afternoon of enjoyment as planned. Betty felt like an intruder or voyeur observing a scene. She was not part of this team, and her decision to leave caused that degree of separation to feel like the width of the Grand Canyon.

Jeremy had understood very clearly from Susan that he was not to push Betty or force her decision until Monday. He had received a call from his friend Bart Hartley that morning and Bart seemed rather smug on the phone when Jeremy confirmed that his offer had not sparked an immediate interest for Betty. His second call of the morning from David did not fare much better, but instead of being smug with her response, David was clearly irritated and ended the call on a bit of an angry tone. It was hardly Jeremy's fault that Betty was not quick to accept the MDP offer.

He was only trying to be honest with her and pray, that retirement would truly be in his immediate future. Susan's car accident had given them both a fright and even without Betty's acceptance of the offer, he had decided that morning, that a discussion with Susan this weekend was needed to possibly resign or ask for an early retirement. He had no intention of missing another day with his wife and family and had seen the accident as a wakeup call for the price he was paying working long hours. And for what was he working those long hours? They no longer needed his paycheck. They were more than set financially. What he needed was Susan and his family, and they needed him present, not at the office.

Jeremy had been successful all morning in having limited contact with Betty. He was pleased that while there were some issues putting data into the new system, the staff were willing to resolve those issues, rather than be difficult and work around the software as often happened with change. The celebration of lunch and games was going very well as all of his staff looked happy and relaxed. At least everyone except Betty. He finally approached her carefully. "Are you ok? I know you have lots to think about, but you do not look like you're having fun here at all."

"I know that you are trying very hard to give me space to think. And I really am giving this decision a lot of thought. Perhaps too much thought, as I hardly slept last night. If it is ok with you, I think I am going to head home for the weekend and try to sort this mess of thoughts and feelings that are tumbling around in my head." Betty was trying to look cheerful; it was very unprofessional to allow personal feelings into the workplace and she had made that mistake back in Albany after Peter had left. It was not appropriate at all in her opinion to show herself in an unprofessional way.

"Sure, if you want to do that. I can make an excuse, that you have an appointment. Just remember one thing please. I will respect whatever decision you make and am available to answer questions or just talk on the weekend. Susan and I cherish your friendship, so that will not change either with your decision, so take any of those thoughts out of the pros and cons list or equation you are using to make your decision." Jeremy was sorry that he had put her in an obviously tough spot. That had never been his intention. He truly believed this was a great opportunity, but only if it was great for her personally as well.

Betty smiled and squeezed his hand as a sign of friendly affection. "I know you both mean well and really appreciate hearing you will not think less of me for my decision. I promised Susan I would take the weekend, and truly give it time. I promise only to do that. I will see you Monday, and thanks for the cover." With that last comment, Betty gathered her bag and left the bar to grab a taxi back to the condo. She did not even say goodbye to her co-workers. Most were involved with games or conversations and would likely not even notice her absence for some time.

She stared out the window of the taxi on the way home. Funny, she thought to herself, she had actually thought of the condo as home. Her only homes before had been her parent's home, and then with Peter. As the taxi made its way through the city, she realised that the path was very familiar. Shops, cross streets, neighbourhoods and directions were as known as Albany, where until 5 months ago she had spent most of her life, with the exception of university. If she chose to stay in Miami, she could buy a car here and not rely on transit, taxi or other people giving her a ride. She could drive herself, and offer others a ride if necessary.

Chapter 19

Betty knew Julia would be wrapping up work, so it was safe to call on a late Friday afternoon. "Hey friend! You have no idea how much I needed to hear your voice and miss you!"

Julia smiled on the other end of the phone miles away. The months that Betty had been away had been both exciting and a bit lonely missing her best friend. "Well, hey yourself! I miss you so much as well. How did the implementation week go?"

Betty continued on their normal conversation for heading home to relax on a Friday evening. "My week has been crazy, and when I say crazy, it is the literal term and not just figuratively. I have so much to catch you up on and a twist at work that I could really use a sounding board for assistance."

Julia was actually at home, and not at the office as Betty assumed. She was scrambling, having tried on her fourth outfit. "Crazy excitement can be wonderful, and I will most definitely be your sounding board, just not tonight. You remember me mentioning Jackson from that co-firm we used for an audit this year?" This was more of a statement rather than a question on Julia's end as she continued. "Well, he asked me to dinner a few times during the audit, just professional, but by the end, we were friends, and then he called me again when the audit was finished. We have been seeing each other since and he is taking me to meet his parents for dinner, over in Maple Grove. They rebuilt the old family cottage and have retired there. It is a huge step for me. Crap! He is picking me up in about 5 minutes!"

Betty could hear the panic in Julia's voice and found herself being the voice of reason, rather than the one needing assurance. "Wow, I remember you mentioning him, but where have I been with it getting to the point of meeting his parents?"

"Well, last weekend was a rather big turning point for us and he really wants me to meet them tonight and then we will have dinner with my parents on Sunday, if all goes well. I have no idea what to wear!" Julia was considering another outfit change.

Betty gulped with the update, apparently, she was not the only one that had held back on details of last weekend. But, then perhaps she had not given Julia time to tell her, with total focus on Jennifer at the condo. "Tell me two things. Did Jackson say casual or formal? Second, what are you wearing right now?"

Julia took a deep breath. Betty was indeed the voice of reason. "He said casual as they are retired and live on the lake. I have on black twill pants that are dressier than jeans, but not dress pants. And a light green cotton shirt with a beige cardigan sweater." Julia was taking another turn in the mirror as she described the garments.

"This sounds perfect, now put those small gold hoops in your ears and that tiny Peridot necklace your parents gave you for your high school graduation. It is simple but still very classy. Wear your Coach black flats, that you got here on your last trip. They are nice but also casual and wear either black socks or green to match your shirt if you can. If his mum is a fashionista, she will pick up on the colours and if she does not you will still feel great." Betty was thinking through Julia's wardrobe for any other changes, but found this very nice for the time they had.

"Thanks so much for your input." Julia was moving around to finish the last touches as Betty had ordered. "I will call you tomorrow morning, or maybe afternoon… Who knew two CPAs could create so much passion." Julia finished with a giggle as the doorbell signalled Jackson's arrival.

Betty heard the bell on her end of the phone as a sign to let Julia go. "Take a few deep breaths before you get out of the car and just enjoy your dinner. If they do not like you, then you and Jackson can decide what to do going forward. Do not borrow trouble trying to please them by being something you are not. Jackson sounds wonderful, so I am thinking they are likely nice as well."

"You are the best! I miss you so much and promise to call tomorrow. Love you!" Julia was already rushing to open the door to Jackson.

"I love you too! Have a great night. Bye-bye." Betty barely heard the bye from Julia as she ended the call. She wished the best for Julia, but was slightly sad and annoyed that her friend was in a relationship and would not be as available as the two had been before. It was also surprising to now realise that her relationship with Peter had never changed her time with Julia. She and Peter rarely went on dates and had just slid into living together. She was starting to see that her relationship with Peter had been more of a roommate with sexual benefits, rather than a loving and intimate partnership.

This realisation was surfacing because of her feelings for David, that was obvious, but she was still stunned to realise the wasted years with Peter and then the grieving when he left. She would surely grieve over her lost love with David, but the feelings were at least worth the grief, even if they were only one sided. She had learned the difference in relationships and that was a lesson, while horribly painful, had been very worthwhile in her mind.

She wished Julia well in her mind as she placed a call to her parents. The details of the weekend with David would remain with her, but the decision for the job offer from Jeremy was clearly in her dad's wheelhouse. He would approach the offer in his very logical way and at least provide that clear perspective towards her final decision.

Chapter 20

David stood in the kitchen of his home having his appearance assessed by four women and three men. It had been a week of back-to-back meetings that had consumed his time and energy, that was still very much an issue from the Jimsonweed poisoning 7 days ago. He had tried to hold everything together on Monday morning, but by the end of the meeting with the regulator he was happy to have Bill Rhodes and Josh present, to ensure he walked out of the office without falling over. Bill had skilfully handled the regulator's questions and their follow up process to clear all charges, but his presence was also required with the Police and District Attorney for the charges against Cameron Lauther and his father.

On the drive back to the house for lunch on Monday, Josh had risked his career by suggesting David call his parents. Bill would be handling the legal aspects, but there were many business-related decisions that David would have to make as well. His father was the only person capable of these decisions for the family business, other than David himself. Grudgingly, David had agreed and had sat in his kitchen surrounded by his Miami family of staff and fortified with half of the meal prepared by Sally. He called Italy.

His parents had arrived on Tuesday and between their assistance, Pirro's care and Sally's cooking, today was the first day he had woken up feeling almost human and back to his own strength. His parents had attended every meeting, Josh had never left his side outside of the house. Sally and his mother had conspired over every morsel of food or drink that entered his system and he was sure that Pirro was reporting every exit from his system. But he had to admit that the attention was appreciated and he was continually thankful, even when irritated with their fussing, for all the care he received.

His mother was one to state the obvious on Wednesday evening when being tired and cranky he had snapped at everyone in the kitchen. "Celestino Davide you apologise immediately, this is your family you are insulting! These people may be in your employ but family could not love you more!" It had been the tears in his mother's eyes while she scolded him, that had him gathering her in his arms and resting his head on her shoulder just as he had done as a little boy. His mother was always right and once he composed himself by his mother's strength, he had made the rounds to each person in the kitchen to apologise for this outburst.

It was his father that had come to his room later in the evening and sat on the opposite side of the bed, just as he had when he read a bedtime story in his childhood. His father did not carry a book but still had a story to tell David. "You know sometimes it is trauma that causes us to wake up and look at what is right in front of us."

"I know that Papi, and I made sure to be sincere in my apology to everyone in the house again, before I came upstairs. If I did not have such a loyal staff, I might not have survived this poisoning. I know the blessing I have with each of them." David was sincere as he looked at his father.

"I am happy to hear you say that. We have also cared for our staff as family and it makes your mother and I very happy to see that you are doing the same here in Florida. But there is one other that you are not mentioning or thanking." The older Davide Baffa wanted to make his son really think as well as hear a story.

"I am very grateful to Ms. McDowall for all she did and is doing to sort out this mess. I will ensure that she is properly thanked and compensated for her loyalty." David was attempting to display that only a professional relationship existed with Betty.

"Ms. McDowall, is it?" Davide senior said with a snort. "I believe the young lady's name is *Betty* and that you owe her much more than thanks and compensation."

"Your right again Papi, I owe her my life." David was uncomfortable being reminded just how much he owed Betty.

"Just your life son? How about your heart?" Davide senior responded in a very quiet voice.

"What do you mean my heart? Why do I owe her my heart?" David was confused with where his father was going with his question.

"I have watched you since walking in that door and holding you close to my heart as a father should hold his son. I felt the strong beat of your heart against mine and gave thanks to God that you were healthy. You were tired and busy with meetings this week, with which I was more than happy to provide my limited assistance and guidance. But, Celestino no one in this house, including your mother and I, are blind to your heart, now belonging for a woman, who appears to be very deserving of not only accepting it, but caring for it, for many years to come." Davide had said his peace and now sat to watch the feelings and emotions play out on his son's face and eyes. His beautiful *Anima Mia*, she was rarely wrong in these matters of the heart and truly was his soul.

"Papi, I do have feelings for her, you are right. But are they true or just a result of a very stressful weekend. I am not even sure what she feels. She cared for me, followed the ruse with the staff and then back into her home and workplace to continue helping. I tried to talk to her on Sunday before she left, but there was no time and there has been no time since. I have been advised by Josh and his team that I should have no contact with Betty until this is all resolved. Cameron being picked up by the police and held for questioning is a huge relief but Josh says until we have the father and other son in police custody, I cannot put her at risk. My only option is to wait until Josh says it is safe to talk to her." David had almost pleaded with his father to have a different solution than the no-contact outlined by Josh.

Davide smiled at this son. "Josh is right and we must follow his guidance, but when all is finished, you will go to her and make everything right."

"And what if she says she does not feel the same or rejects my love? What do I do then Papi?" David was worried she would slam the door in his face and run back to Albany.

"Ah, then we will send your mother." Davide smiled and patted his son cheek, just like he had when David was a boy. His son was healthy and finally in love. He would report that bambinos would not be far off in the future.

Now here, David stood in his own kitchen, being inspected prior to his drive to Betty's condo. He would drive himself with Naldo following at a distance to watch for a tail, and Josh to follow Naldo for added measure. He had the entire drive to practice his speech and think about the changes to his house and business that would be required, within the coming year.

David parked a few spaces away from Betty's door. He did not want her to have a chance look out the window and not even open the door to him. He gathered his items and did one last check of his pocket before exiting the car and locking it.

Just as he was approaching the front steps a pizza delivery car zipped to the curb and a driver quickly emerged, to extract a pie from his back seat where the insulated bag held the deliveries. David called to him and the young man bumped his head startled of being addressed by someone on the street. David confirmed the delivery was for Betty and accepted it, with payment and very generous tip for the bumped head. "Can you stay at the curb until she answers the door?"

"Dude for that tip, I can wait as long as you want!" The driver would have happily sacrificed the remaining two deliveries as the tip more than covered his cost of two pies.

"Not necessary, just until she opens the door." David ascended and then stood just to the side of the front door security viewer. She would see the car and know it was her pizza delivery.

Betty opened the front door seeing the car and box through the viewer. She had started to make a salad for dinner and then chose to splurge on a pizza. The cash for the pie and tip sitting beside the door was scooped up as she opened the door to accept the box. There was a good movie on and she was happy to zone out from the week while munching on pepperoni and extra cheese.

Betty noticed the car drive away when she opened the door. The box remained at her door along with a delivery of long stem pink roses and a bottle of red wine. But it was the face that was behind the roses that had her breath catching in her throat.

David had peeked out from behind the roses and after seeing the startled reaction from Betty had to take a deep breath himself for assurance. "I have your pizza and few other items. May I come in?"

Betty was slowly recovering from the initial shock and while happy to see him plus all the extra items felt a bit of anger rising with the pleasure. She would not be used by this man, regardless of the puppy eyes. He had taken many liberties last weekend, but no contact for the week and then the job offer from Jeremy, had left her thinking they were done. Showing up with roses (pink was her favourite) and wine would not be enough for a simple slide into her home to have his way. Betty pushed her shoulders back a bit and raised her chin, to show some defiance. "Maybe." And to further reiterate her point of irritation offered the money for her pizza. "My pizza can come in for sure."

"Can the flowers?" David saw the set of her shoulder change and knew it would not be simple. When Betty nodded in agreement to the flowers, he smiled and continued. "How about the wine?" Which he received another nod of agreement. And finally, the big one. "How about me Betty, may I also come in?" David so wanted to add a smile to his question, but her expression of surprise had not yet changed to happiness at seeing him, so thought it best to remain sombre.

"Fine, but if the roses wilt and the wine is not good, then you are out delivery boy." Betty wanted to smile. She wanted to shout with joy at seeing him. She wanted to throw her arms around his neck and kiss him with every ounce of passion she had. But to do so would be dangerous and after this week, she had had enough danger. Instead, she turned to allow him to enter and motioned for him to continue through to the kitchen area, as she closed the front door.

Betty followed David to the kitchen and while he stayed at the bar setting down the three items, Betty moved into the kitchen. "Since you have an update from both Jennifer and Jeremy on my week, how about you fill me in on yours." Betty was determined to remain unattached and set about the tasks of a vase, dishes, and wine glasses.

David took a deep breath to settle himself. Sally and his mother had been clear this may be tougher than he envisioned, but he had left the house with hope and was still clinging to that thought like a lifeline. "I am feeling almost fully recovered, largely thanks to you!"

"I can see that, and am happy for you." Nothing more, no smile or longing look from his eyes. Fine, Betty thought as she continued to look for a corkscrew. Stay busy and detached!

"Right." David felt the response and detachment like a slap. Then heard his mother's voice to tell Betty everything. "I was so weak on Monday that Josh made me call my parents. I did not have the strength to go to the meetings and fully comprehend what was being said. It was the first time in my life that I was completely depended, first on you for my care

197

and then my staff for everything. It was a rather humbling experience."

Betty had begun arranging the roses, and hearing his last statement finally looked up. Still no smile but she could feel the heat of tears forming. "I am sorry, I did not stop to think it was a tough week for you as well."

David came around the corner of the island and reached for Betty. If she reached back, it was a sign of acceptance, if not he had much more work to do. But he was rewarded with Betty reaching back.

Betty met his embrace and briefly saw the added moisture in his eyes just before he lowered his mouth to capture hers in a kiss so soft, she was not sure he was truly touching her lips.

David withdrew his lips and moved to her cheek. His arms had encircled her with such strength and warmth that Betty found herself gasping for breath.

Instead of releasing her as expected he continued to hold her tight as the entire week poured out. "The advice for no contact with you, for your safety, was worse than being ill. All I did was endure meetings and force myself to eat before sleeping. Had my parents not been present for meetings, I am sure I would have made numerous mistakes. But the worst, was not being with you, not talking to you, not hearing your voice."

Betty could not believe what she was hearing and feeling. His absence was to protect her? How could that be? Finally finding her voice and not wanting to be released from his embrace she responded. "I am glad your parents and everyone at the house was there for you. I thought you wanted nothing to do with me, as there was no contact all week."

David was processing her response and found himself fumbling to in his pocket. "Nothing to do with you? Are you kidding? I spent 48 hours close to you, trusting you, and have never felt so close to someone in my life!" His fingers finally found their objective and he extracted the antique jeweller's box. He lowered himself to one knee and held out the box on the palm of his hand and opened with his other. "Elizabeth McDowell, you may have saved my life but you stole my heart. I fell in love listening to your voice in my bathroom and am asking you to share the rest of our lives together, so I can hear your voice for the remainder of my life. Please say you will do me the honour of being my only love and wife forever."

David had been staring up at Betty, with eyes so intense, that the puppy look was gone. This was not a joke, or apology, or anything but a huge diamond antique ring winking at her from the glare of the kitchen light. David loved her! The weekend had been just as emotional for him as her, and now he was asking her to be his wife. Her voice was choked in her throat and the tears brimming from before had let go of their barrier to flow freely down her face.

"I am still not that healthy and this pose is getting shaky, can I get a, yes?" David now had a lovely shy smile with the puppy look making a return.

Betty pulled his outstretched arm holding the ring as a gesture to rise and once steady, then stood on her toes while throwing both arms around his neck just as she had wanted to at the front door with his arrival. Just before dragging him down to a long-desired kiss she softly whispered, "Yes."

David finally surfaced from the kiss feeling like a man that had finally found water after days of thirst. He looked at

Betty's flushed face and brilliant brown eyes that he wanted to see forever. "I never knew that my purchase of MDP would also be a pipeline to love and romance in a weekend." David dipped to her for another long and scintillating kiss. Betty was finding it hard to stand when David broke away and looked at her very seriously. "Just one more thing… Jennifer is pregnant, we will have a busy house, Mrs Baffa."

"Yes, we will indeed, Mr Baffa!"

Printed in the USA
CPSIA information can be obtained
at www.ICGtesting.com
LVHW050739100124
768556LV00009B/116

9 781398 485198